Lyrical Symphony

REGINA ANN FAITH

ISBN: 978-1-7371753-2-2

Library of Congress Control Number:

Any reference to historical events, real people, or real places are used fictitiously. Names, characters, and places are products of the author's imagination.

Edited By: One Word Editing, https://www.onewordediting.com

Front Cover Design by Diana T. Calcado, www.triumphbookcovers.com

Formatting by Dark Ink Designs www.darkinkpublication.com

First Printed Edition, 2023

Dance is my art. The floor is my canvas and I am the brush. ***(Unknown)***

Dancing is my drug, music is my dealer. ***(Unknown)***

When in doubt, dance it out. ***(Unknown)***

Only when I'm dancing do I feel this free. ***(Unknown)***

Also By Regina Faith

<u>Artistic Series</u>

Artistic Love In The Psych Ward

Artistic Soulmates

<u>The Love Sick Series</u>

Illicit Dose Of Scars

Illicit Dose Of Chaos

<u>Standalone</u>

Lyrical Symphony

CHAPTER 1
Lyric

I was practicing my dance moves in the living room when my roommate, Sierra, walked in.

"Lyric, all you do is practice. Eat, sleep, and practice," she said in a huff.

I ignored her and kept dancing. Sierra knew I had no time for distractions. I was a professional dancer who had to be serious about my career. I joined the New York City Rhythm in Motion Dance Troupe straight out of high school and had been dancing with them ever since. We'd traveled all over the US and overseas. I'd made a lot of great memories dancing with the troupe. Our instructor, Sloane Embers, was like a second mom to me. She knew I had potential, even at eighteen. Now twenty-five, I was more confident than ever about my choice of career. And no one, not even my roommate, was going to talk badly or down to me about it.

"Well, no one can be like you. The infamous tattoo artist," I said as I began stretching to cool down.

Sierra was thirty and a sought-after tattoo artist. She had olive skin and light-green eyes. She dyed her hair a different color every few months. Right now, it was burgundy with black highlights and was cut in a medium-length, asymmetrical bob. She also had a ton of tattoos, which she had been collecting since she turned eighteen. Her favorite tattoo was a small butterfly on the inside of her wrist. In the few years she'd been a tattoo artist, Sierra had built most of her clientele through Instagram and TikTok. She'd had a variety of clients, from the straitlaced businessman to the hardcore punk rocker and everyone in between.

Sierra was a brilliant tattooist; her drawing skills were impeccable. She'd asked me a few times if I wanted her to draw me a dance-inspired tattoo to ink somewhere on my body. Each time, I said I'd think about it. Truthfully, I was scared of getting something so permanent on my body. Maybe one day I would get the courage, just not right now.

"Of course they can't," Sierra replied to my comment. "No one can tattoo like me. And I'm sure no one could charge the rates I do."

"Bitch," I said.

She curtsied. "The one and only."

We busted out laughing at each other.

"So what's on your agenda today?" I asked Sierra, moving from the floor to sit on the couch.

"I have a few appointments today, so I have to go into the shop. But I wanted to ask if you're free to help out at the shop for a couple of shifts while Everly's on vacation. I had a few other people in mind, but you know I always like to ask you first before I go with someone else."

"A couple of shifts? Umm . . . I will be practicing for an upcoming show, and you know how strict Sloane is. But if I can, I want to help you out. I'll let you know, okay?"

"Yeah. Just let me know, as soon as possible."

"I'm getting ready to go into the studio now, so I should have an answer for you when I get back."

"Alright." Sierra walked toward her bedroom.

I got up off the couch and ventured to my own bedroom. It was my sacred space. Sierra's room was cluttered, but I loved the minimalist look. On my hardwood floor, I had a simple gold rug with fringe on the ends. Next to the rug was a tall, green plant that my mom had given me when I'd moved in. I was surprised it had lived this long. I usually forgot to water it every day, like I was supposed to. My bed was a queen with white sheets and a few different-colored throw blankets I used for my comforter. The walls were white, and I had some family and dance pictures hanging up, scattered around strategically.

I climbed on my bed, grabbed my journal off the night-stand, and pulled out the pen from the glittery gold holder. There was enough time to write a few lines before I had to leave for the dance studio. Along with the plant, my mom had also given me a set of journals to document my dance journey and life in general. I wrote today's date and began writing my thoughts. I jotted down a few sentences about my hopes for this new performance the dance troupe will embark on, then closed the journal. I decided to freshen up before heading to the studio. I went to the bathroom to wash my face. I looked in the mirror. My tawny-beige skin was looking great today. But my hair—my sandy-brown hair—was in desperate need of a trim. I liked wearing it straight because it was easier to maintain, but it had gotten way too long, even for when I wore it in all its curly ringlet glory. I put on my leotard and yoga pants, and I grabbed my dance bag and threw it over my shoulder.

"I'm heading to the studio now," I yelled toward Sierra's bedroom.

"Okay, have fun," she yelled back.

EXPRESSION OF DANCE was in the art district in downtown Manhattan, only a few blocks from Sierra's tattoo shop, Underneath the Skin. We rode together to work occasionally, but it was very rare that we went in at the same times. I had to remember to ask Sloane the times of our practices for this upcoming show so I could see if I could help Sierra out. It would be a little extra money in my pocket, which I'd be grateful for.

When I arrived at the studio, I parked my car, grabbed my dance bag, and walked into the building. The receptionist, Ms. Brandi Leigh, greeted me as soon as I walked through the door. She was a feisty woman in her fifties. We had coined her as the "Feisty Dance Mom." Ms. Brandi never married and enjoyed treating the dancers like the daughters she never had. She gave us advice about whatever we needed help with. Whether it be about boys, makeup, or things we were too shy or embarrassed to talk about.

Ms. Brandi acted as our confidante, but if it was detrimental to us, she always repeated the same statement: "Even though you are telling me this and I respect your privacy, I think you should talk to a professional about what you are going through." She pointed us in the right direction by giving us resources to contact regarding our situations. She was the best. Many of us came from families that didn't pay much attention to us, so Ms. Brandi's words of encouragement, correction, and guidance were a lifesaver. We were all so grateful to her for listening to us in our times of need.

"Hey, Lyric. How are you doing?" she asked, smiling.

"I'm doing well. How are you doing, Ms. Brandi?"

"I'm doing well too."

"That's good," I said before heading to the dance room.

I entered the room to find the other dancers stretched out on the floor or positioned at the barre. I was so glad I'd stretched before I arrived. Now I could do a light warm-up before we started learning the new routine for the upcoming performance. After I put my dance shoes on, I dropped my bag next to the wall. Then I sat on the floor and began my light stretch.

"Hey, Lyric. Are you ready to learn the new routine for the performance?" Mei asked beside me.

"I am. I'm so excited about learning this routine," I said.

Mei was thirty—five years older than me. She had an interesting story as she was a child of Chinese immigrants. Her parents had moved to America shortly before she was born. They'd wanted to give her the life they didn't have growing up. They had enrolled her in a private elementary school and in dance classes. She'd gone to a public high school and graduated top of her class. She'd gone on to college to get a degree in dance performance. Mei had joined the dance troupe right out of college and had been dancing with Sloane ever since.

After our brief exchange, Sloane entered the room and started to set up the music for us to begin. Sloane Embers was in her midforties with short, strawberry-blonde hair and blue eyes. She was the premier dance instructor in New York City. She'd grown up with parents that were entertainers. So she told us that, naturally, she'd gravitated toward the entertainment industry and had settled on becoming a dance instructor. Over the years, her dance teams had won a slew of awards and metals. She was the best of the best, and I was so grateful to be a part of a dynamic dance team. Us girls were not just dancers; we were a tight-knit family.

"Alright." Sloane clapped her hands to get our attention after she finished setting up the first song we were going to dance to. "We will be performing two dance routines for this upcoming show. One routine will be a lyrical dance that's ethereal and haunting. The other routine will be influenced by jazz and hip-hop. It has an up-tempo beat and quick and fast movements. Are you girls ready for the challenge?"

All of us looked at each other and nodded in agreement, then nodded at Sloane. I was ready for the performance. I couldn't wait to live and breathe these dance routines.

"Okay then. Let's get started." Sloane turned on the music and began teaching us the lyrical dance.

We practiced learning the routine for two hours. It was indeed hauntingly beautiful with a lot of slow, meticulously fluid body movements. As we moved together, everyone seemed to get the flow of the dance and felt the music in their veins. It was pure perfection.

"Let's cool down for fifteen minutes," Sloane finally said, changing the music to a slower-tempo song.

After we did some cool-down stretches and a few breathing exercises, the dancers gathered their belongings. I said a quick goodbye to Mei, distracted by my need to ask Sloane when the upcoming practices would be.

"Sloane," I said when everyone else was gone.

"Yes, Lyric," she said.

"I just wanted to know if there are any special times for practicing the routines we are learning." I was hoping that there weren't any practices so I could fill in at Sierra's shop. I stood there waiting for Sloane's answer.

She was busy fiddling with the radio and the speakers, then she turned to face me. "No, no special times as of right now. Just during the class. Although, when it's closer to the performance date, I will call more practices. But you have time. Why, what's up?"

"Well, my roommate needs help at her shop, and I offered to help her out, but I don't want it to conflict with my practice times."

"Oh, okay. Just let me know if you can't be in attendance, and I can set up a time where we can do a one-on-one practice session," Sloane said.

"Thank you. I appreciate that and will let you know. It's only for a couple of shifts."

"No problem. A couple of shifts is nothing. You should have the routines down pat in no time. It will be fine. Like I said, we can set up a one-on-one practice session if need be." Sloane smiled.

I smiled back, grabbed my belongings, and left the class. I decided to walk the few blocks to Sierra's tattoo shop.

I WALKED UP to the tattoo shop's reception desk. "Hey, Everly. Is Sierra available?"

"She's in the middle of doing a tattoo. She should be finished soon though," Everly said.

Everly was thirty, the same age as Sierra. She had long, dark-purple hair and light-brown eyes. Tattoos covered her arms, and a silver hoop ring adorned her nose. She wore black leather jeans, a graphic tee crop top, and black platform combat boots.

"So, can you fill in for me?" Everly asked.

"I can fill in for you, but I need to talk to Sierra first. I want to confirm that she didn't find anyone else."

"Okay." Everly thumbed through the appointment book.

I took a seat and waited for Sierra to finish tattooing her client. Underneath the Skin was a mix of glamour and grunge—the two sides of Sierra's personality. She was into the grungy style, which her clothes and tattoos reflected most of the time, but she could still slay in a dress and heels. I was surprised when she incorporated that glamour aspect into her shop's decor. But it worked so well.

"I fucking love it," a guy said while walking into the lobby. One arm sported a bandage, likely covering his new tattoo.

I stood. Sierra walked to the reception desk and told Everly what I assumed was the price of the guy's tattoo. She talked to Everly, then shifted her focus to me.

"Oh, hey Lyric. How was your practice?" she asked.

"It was good. I stopped by to tell you I'm able to fill in for Everly, if you still need me to."

"Yes. Great! I'm glad. That's definitely a weight off my shoulders," Sierra said.

"Thanks for being willing to fill in for me while I'm on vacation, Lyric," Everly said, looking at me and smiling.

"You're welcome. I'm happy to help in any way I can." I smiled back.

Everly handed the guy a receipt, and he glanced my way. "My name is Zane, by the way. And you are?"

"I'm Lyric, Sierra's roommate."

"Well, it's nice to meet you, Lyric." He looked me up and down. "Do you dance?"

"Yes. How can you tell?"

"You've got that look about you." He smiled. "I'm in a hip-hop dance troupe called Drop the Beat. We perform all over New York City."

"Oh, okay," I said, sort of matter-of-factly.

"You don't believe me? I was just telling Sierra about our recent performance."

"He was," Sierra said, giving me a look as if to say, *He's cute, go for it.*

Zane was cute. He had blond hair and blue eyes. His baggy jeans, sneakers, and a graphic tee gave off a skater vibe, which was cool. I was just not ready or in the mood to talk, or flirt, with anyone right now.

"I believe you. That's cool," I said.

"So . . . what kind of dance do you do?" Zane asked.

"I do a little bit of everything. But I love lyrical dance."

"Oh, that's cool. Lyric, can I ask you something?"

I eyed him warily. "It depends. If it's on a date, no. I'm not interested."

"Lyric," Sierra scolded and cut her eyes at me. To Zane, she said, "Don't mind my roommate. She clearly has issues with knowing when to shut up and just go with the flow."

"I see that," Zane said and then laughed. "Anyway, I wanted to see if both of you are free to go to a goth concert next Saturday. The name of the band is Nightmarish Daydreams. I know the lead singer, Axel. He is a real cool, chill guy. And it's not a date." He gave me a reassuring look.

"Well, I don't know. I—"

"Of course, we would love to," Sierra cut me off.

"Great. Do you have a piece of paper? I can write down the details," Zane said.

"Here you go." Everly handed him paper and a pen.

When Zane had his back to us, I quickly glared at Sierra. She stared back and shrugged. Zane wrote the information, handed Sierra the paper, and off he went.

"You need to relax, Lyric," Sierra said after he left.

"Yeah, okay." I rolled my eyes.

"It's only a concert. Even if he just asked you to go, I

would have pushed you into going. Life doesn't only revolve around dance. You don't want to spend your whole life dancing to wake up one day and regret you never took the time to get to know someone and experience love."

"Maybe you have a point," I said reluctantly.

"Fuck yeah, I do."

CHAPTER 2

Xenia

The Briar Convention Center was in downtown Manhattan. It was shaped like a dome with glass window panels covering the entire circumference of the roof. Today was the final practice. The concert was in a week. Our orchestra, Sacred Ethereal Symphony, conducted by Mr. Charles Stewart, had been asked to be the opening act for Nightmarish Daydreams, a local goth band. When Mr. Charles had told the orchestra about this opportunity, we'd almost flipped. It wasn't every day we got to open for a musical act, let alone a goth band.

We were all situated in the pit below the stage, awaiting the instructions of Mr. Charles. He dressed very eccentrically for his sixty-four years. His peppered gray hair enhanced his outfit even more. He recently shared a story with us that years ago, he'd wanted to form and conduct an orchestra that focused on ethereal orchestral compositions. There were not a lot of orchestras that played the type of music Mr. Charles wanted to play. So, he'd put pen to paper and started creating his own ethereal compositions. He told us that over the years, he had written over one thousand orchestral pieces. We were going to play four of those pieces in our set opening for Nightmarish Daydreams.

"From the top," Mr. Charles said, standing in front of us holding his baton. "One . . . two . . . three." He raised the baton and cued us in.

We started playing the first composition, "Haunted Melody," which had a slow tempo and was a cello- and viola-based piece. The first and second violins had the harmony. As a first violinist, I was used to having the melody. When I looked up at Mr. Charles to cue the first violins in, he was waving his baton with very pronounced movements.

"You guys are nailing this transition," he declared.

It was obvious he was pleased at the way we were all blending together as we played. It sounded heavenly echoing off the walls of the empty auditorium.

After we finished practicing the other three compositions, Mr. Charles invited the entire orchestra out to lunch for some bonding time. He asked us for a consensus on where we should eat, and we all decided on Skyline Diner. As the name suggested, whether walking toward the diner or sitting in a booth looking out the windows, there was a magnificent view of the New York skyline.

As I started to pack up my violin, I shot a glance over at my good friend Brielle, who was doing the same thing. She was a twenty-seven-year-old Latina who'd grown up around Spanish culture and music. That was all she'd known until she'd discovered classical music. After hearing an orchestra play for the first time, she'd wanted to learn how to play the violin. Brielle's parents had encouraged her to take up the instrument. They had been excited to discover she was a quick learner. She'd later joined our orchestra, where we'd met and hit it off so well.

"Hey, Bri, ready for the concert?" I asked.

"So ready. My extended family is flying in from Mexico to see my performance," Brielle explained as she pushed her long honey-brown curls out of her face.

"From Mexico . . . wow. I wish some of my family in China would come to see me perform."

"Maybe one day they will, Xenia." I could tell Brielle meant her encouraging words.

"Ladies, we're heading over to Skyline Diner now," Mr. Charles said, interrupting our conversation.

I looked around. Everyone else had already packed up and left. Mr. Charles was probably lingering around wondering what was taking Brielle and me so long to pack up.

"Oh, I'm sorry. I didn't realize we were the only ones left in here," I told him with a light chuckle.

"Here we come," Brielle chimed in.

We both finished packing up and hurried out to our cars.

LUCKILY TRAFFIC WASN'T that bad, and I got to the diner quickly. When I walked inside, I looked around for the members of the orchestra. I spotted them, walked over to their table, and sat in an empty seat next to Brielle.

"Boy, you had to drive like a speed demon to beat me here," I said to Brielle.

"I did leave slightly before you," Bri stated matter-of-factly.

"Okay, fair enough." I picked up a menu and started to scan through it. "Did you order yet?"

"Yeah, we all ordered our food."

I quickly looked over the menu. I chose what I wanted to eat, then flagged the server down. She came to our table and took my drink and food order.

"I'll put a rush on this so your food can come out with the others," she said, smiling politely. "I'll get your drink as soon as I put the order in, okay?"

"Okay." I nodded.

The server walked away from the table and disappeared into the kitchen. After she left, I focused my attention on the group. They had a lot of different conversations going on at the same time.

"Ladies and gentlemen," Mr. Charles said above the simultaneous chatter.

Everyone immediately stopped their conversations and focused their attention on him.

"We had a wonderful practice today. I think we are more than ready to show up and show out as the opening act for Nightmarish Daydreams. The audience won't know what hit them. I'm so excited to play these pieces and see their reactions."

We nodded in agreement. It was clear we were all excited to play the songs.

"Next week, I want you all to be at the convention center an hour early so we can practice the songs one more time before we go on," he added.

Just then, our food came. The server gave us our plates, and we all ate with minimal conversation. After everyone finished eating, we continued to chat about being the opening act for Nightmarish Daydreams. During the conversation, my cell phone vibrated. It was my mom.

> Mom: Xen, you live twenty minutes away. When are you coming to visit us? You haven't been by to visit us in a while. We miss you.

Me: I'm at lunch right now, but I will swing by afterward, okay?

Mom: Great. We can't wait to see what you've been up to. Love you.

Me: Love you too.

I usually went to my parents' house every other weekend, but I'd been swamped with rehearsals for this upcoming performance. Even though the practices were on the weekdays, they were exhausting, and I just felt like relaxing on the weekends. I didn't want to deal with my parents' endless questioning of what was going on in my life. I knew my parents just wanted to be updated on my life, but I felt they hovered over me when all I wanted was a little space. I wasn't a teenager anymore. I was twenty-five and lived on my own. *Chill out sometimes, folks.* I decided to cut the lunch outing short and head to my parents' house.

"Hey, guys, I'm getting ready to go. Something's come up," I told the group.

"Is everything okay?" Mr. Charles asked, a concerned look on his face.

"Yeah, yeah. Everything's fine," I said. "I'll see you guys tomorrow at the show."

"Yes, of course. Have a great rest of your day," Mr. Charles said.

I said goodbye to Brielle and the rest of the group and left the diner.

ON THE DRIVE TO MY PARENTS' house, I thought about the things they would likely ask me. It'd been a while since I visited them. They would probably want to know what else I'd been doing besides practicing with the orchestra. I didn't owe them an explanation as to why I hadn't visited them. But I had to let them know the reason, because even though I was twenty-five, they still acted like I was fifteen. The need to know my whereabouts and what I was up to hadn't let up. But I got it. I totally got it. Especially being the daughter of Chinese immigrant parents.

I parked my car close to the curb nearest the house, got out, and walked up the cobblestone driveway to the red front door. I rang the doorbell twice. My parents had chosen this house based on the color of the door. In Chinese culture, the color red symbolized happiness, joy, and luck. So, when my parents had seen the door, they hadn't even cared what the inside of the house looked like. My parents had known that this house would bring all the happiness, joy, and luck they needed to survive in America.

I took a step back and waited a few seconds and then rang the doorbell a third time. Soon the door flung open and my mom, Aimee, who everyone called Ai, came out. She gave me the biggest hug.

"Xen, I'm so glad you finally came to visit. Your dad and I have been missing you," my mom said as she continued to hug me.

"Yeah, I've been busy with the orchestra, Mom. We have a show coming up," I told her.

"Of course, well come on in. Tao and Mei are here visiting. I'm sure they want to see you too. Tao . . . Mei . . . Xen is here," my mom yelled into the hallway.

"My little cherry blossom," Aunt Tao yelled back.

"Hey, Aunt Tao," I said. I made my way to the living room where they were all sitting on the couch, no doubt spilling the tea.

"Xen, where have you been?" my cousin Mei asked me when I sat on the couch.

"I've been busy with practices for an upcoming concert. We are opening for a local goth band," I told her excitedly.

"Oh, I totally get that. My dance troupe has a performance coming up as well."

"It's been a while since you saw each other perform," my mom said. "Why don't you see if you can go see Mei perform with her dance troupe and then she can come to your orchestra performance."

"That's a great idea," Aunt Tao chimed in.

"It's settled then. Before you leave, Xen, let us know when the show is, and we'll be there. And, Mei, let us know when your performance is." My mom looked between the both of us.

"Are you guys hungry? I made jiaozi," Aunt Tao said proudly.

Jiaozi was the traditional name for the dish commonly known as Chinese dumplings. Both Aunt Tao and my mom, who were six years apart, made jiaozi every Sunday. It was our favorite Chinese meal. It reminded Mei and me of China and our grandparents, who we both missed so much. The last time we saw our grandparents was at Mei and Qiang's wedding five years ago.

We all got up from the couch and ventured into the kitchen. Mom and Aunt Tao motioned for Mei and me to sit at the table while they fixed our plates. Soon all of us were sitting at the table and eating the delicious dumplings.

"So, Mei, when are you and Qiang planning to have children?" my mom asked.

Mei was chewing, and I saw her visibly swallow. She nervously grabbed her iced tea, took a sip, and set it back on the table. She took a deep breath before addressing the eagerly awaiting future great-aunt and future grandma.

"Well, Qiang and I are really too busy with our careers to think about having kids right now," Mei said.

"I'm ready to be a grandma, Mei." Aunt Tao pouted.

"You aren't getting any younger, Mei. Your mom is right in her readiness to be a grandma," my mom said.

"Well, I will let you know when we plan on telling you that I'm pregnant," Mei said. "But right now, our careers are our priority."

"That's a shame. You were always so stubborn," Aunt Tao said, disappointed.

Mei didn't say anything else. I knew she wasn't going to argue with her mom. Aunt Tao had to realize it was Mei's life and her body, and that Mei is free to do what she pleased, even when her mom didn't agree with her choices. We continued eating without saying a word.

After a few moments, my mom whispered something in Aunt Tao's ear. They looked at me simultaneously.

"I think it's time," my mom announced.

I looked at my mom and Aunt Tao. "Time for what?"

"To discuss your engagement and wedding plans," Aunt Tao stated.

Mei sighed and looked relieved. She was no longer the center of attention in the conversation. "Yes, let's talk about it," Mei stated eagerly.

I sank into my chair. I didn't want to have this conversation, but I knew it was inevitable. I'd known this day would come. I would be married off to a man that my parents chose for me. Even still, I had been in denial about it for the longest time. Even though I dated men here and there, none of them ever lasted. When Mei started dating Qiang on her own, and my family warmed up to him, I felt pressure to find a guy that

I liked so I wouldn't have to marry a stranger, but that hadn't happened. Now here I was, having this discussion with my mom, aunt, and cousin.

"The suitor's name is Jun Lee, and he comes from a well-established Chinese family," my mom explained. "Your dad has been in communication with him and his family. He also sent Jun a picture of you. Jun was very pleased with your photograph and can't wait to meet you."

"Is it too late to for me to find someone I like?" I asked.

"Why? Your mom told me about Jun, and he seems to really like you," Aunt Tao objected.

"Well, Mei found Qiang and they're happily married."

"I got married five years ago, when the dating pool was not like it was today," Mei said. "It's slim pickings out here. I just got lucky, and in the beginning, I thought that wasn't going to be the case."

"Mei is right. Have you seen the guys out here?" Aunt Tao said with a chuckle.

This was a battle that I would never win, so I listened to them speak about Jun and his family, their hopes for me and him, and everything in between. Eventually, I realized I didn't want to be part of this discussion anymore.

After a pause in the conversation, I abruptly changed the subject. "So . . . my performance is in a week's time," I said, hoping they didn't pick up on me not wanting to talk about the engagement and wedding plans.

"What day?" my mom asked.

They hadn't noticed. I was in the clear. "Saturday. Is that a good day for you? Aunt Tao . . . Mei?" I looked between all three of them.

"That's perfect for me," Mei said.

"Yes, that's works for me as well," Aunt Tao said.

"How about you, Mom?" I asked.

"I wouldn't miss it for the world," she said, smiling.

"When's your dance performance, Mei?" Aunt Tao asked.

"In two weeks. It's also on a Saturday," she spoke confidently, like she had forgotten that her mom had called her stubborn a few minutes ago.

"Alright, I'll mark my calendar," Aunt Tao said.

"Me too," my mom chimed in.

Mei then looked at me.

"You know I'll be there," I said, smiling at her. "Hey, listen, I have to get ready to go. I have a few things I need to do this afternoon."

"Oh . . . I understand. The life of a concert violinist," my mom said reassuringly.

"We can't wait to see your performance, Xenia," Aunt Tao chimed in, speaking for Mei as well.

I went around the table and hugged each one of them before leaving.

"See you all next week," I said.

"Bye, Xenia," they said in unison, almost like they'd rehearsed it.

CHAPTER 3
Lyric

I had an interesting dream last night. In it, I saw this beautiful girl when I went to the Nightmarish Daydreams concert. She had long black hair and dark, almond-shaped eyes. I couldn't make out what she was wearing or even if I saw her in the crowd, but she was breath-taking. I caught myself staring at her, biting my lip. I had no clue why because I didn't like girls. But her image burned a hole in my mind. I was frantic, and my heart was beating triple time for her.

As I struggled to open my eyes, I said, "What the fuck?"

I lay in bed with my hand on my chest, trying to calm the beating of my heart. I took several deep breaths. *Inhale, exhale,* I thought. This dream seemed significant. The concert was this evening. I was excited to go, but this dream shook me to the core. I didn't know what to make of it. *Should I talk to Sierra?* I wondered. *Or maybe I'll just wait and see if the dream manifests itself tonight.*

I sat up in bed and tried to smooth out my long, sandy-brown hair that was sticking out every which way on the top of my head. I rubbed the sleep out of my eyes. When I touched my MY BLACK IS BEAUTIFUL sleep shirt, it was soaked with sweat. *Shit*. I grabbed my journal and pen off my nightstand. I wanted to remember and write the dream down while it was fresh in my mind. Even if it didn't manifest at the concert this evening, it didn't mean that it wouldn't in some capacity in the future.

After I finished jotting down the details of the dream in my journal, I got out of bed. I grabbed my robe out of my closet and put it on, wrapping it around me. My stomach was growling, and I couldn't ignore it any longer. I walked into the kitchen. Sierra watched me as I made my way to the pantry. I could feel her eyes following my every move as I made a bowl of oatmeal.

"What?" I said, annoyed.

"Nothing." She bit a piece of a mini chocolate-chip muffin.

"It's something."

"Never mind. Are you ready for the concert tonight?" she asked.

I went quiet, reminiscing about the dream I just had. *Am I ready for the concert? Yes and no?* I was not ready to face Zane, who clearly wanted to fuck me. I was pretty sure he invited both Sierra and I to the concert just to make me feel comfortable about going. I also wasn't totally sure if I was ready to see if this dream was going to somehow manifest itself tonight.

"Earth to Lyric," Sierra said, throwing a piece of her muffin at me.

"What the hell, Sierra!"

"Sorry. You zoned out there for a minute. I had to snap you out of it somehow. Umm . . . the concert?" she reiterated.

"Yes. What about it?" I said, puzzled.

"Are you ready for it?" Sierra shook her head. "Are you okay?"

"Oh, yes. I'm ready for it. I'm fine," I said, trying to convince myself.

"I'm stoked for it. I looked the band up and listened to a few of their songs. They're really good!"

"Oh, okay. What type of music do they play?"

"It's more of a haunting-melodies and loud-guitar-riffs kind of band. The lead singer, Axel, has a very distinctive singing voice. It's hard to describe, but it's soothing."

I sat at the table across from Sierra with my bowl of oatmeal. She pulled up her Spotify list and played me some of their songs so I could get an idea of what they sounded like. They certainly did have haunting melodies and loud guitar riffs. I liked their songs. I could envision a chilled and relaxed concert atmosphere. Axel's voice was unlike any other singer I'd heard before. It was mysteriously soft and beautiful in some songs, but loud and throaty in other songs. His voice was interesting to say the least.

THE CONCERT STARTED at eight in the evening. When it was time to start getting ready, I decided to borrow Sierra's black jeans that were ripped at the knees and to wear fishnet stockings underneath with a black halter top, blue denim jacket, and my black platform Converse shoes. She did say I had to look like I was going to a goth concert. I put on red lipstick and my hair up in a high, messy bun. I really liked this look. After we were dressed, Sierra texted Zane to tell him that we were on our way to the convention center. He texted her back that he had the tickets and would meet us in front of the building.

When we arrived at the convention center, it was packed with people waiting for the concert to begin. Sierra and I spotted Zane. He was wearing baggy jeans and a Nightmarish Dreams band shirt. His blond hair was spiked on top of his head.

"You girls made it," Zane said when we walked up to him.

"Yes, we did. It's packed. Are their concerts usually this crowded?" Sierra asked.

"They have a pretty good following. They get a lot of plays on Spotify and YouTube." He looked my way and smiled. "You look nice."

"Thank you," I said feeling self-conscious from his hungry eyes.

"Ready to go in?" Sierra asked, anxiously.

"Sure. I've got front-row seats, and I'm able to get us in early to meet the band," Zane said excitedly.

"Really? Awesome. Well, what are we waiting here for? Let's go," I said.

We followed Zane to the ticket booth where he showed the agent our tickets and early-access passes. I was excited and nervous to see the concert. The dream I had last night was permanently embedded in my brain like a tattoo. Even though I didn't know what the night would bring, I was excited to see the band in concert. Zane, Sierra, and I entered the building. People were standing around, waiting for the concert to start and chatting among themselves. Almost everyone was dressed in black, but there was some red thrown in the mix. Posters of the band were scattered all over the walls of the building. We made our way through the crowd, and we soon reached a room where the band was finishing up practicing before going on stage.

"Hey, Axel. I'm stoked for the show tonight," Zane said after they finished playing. He gave Axel a fist bump.

"I'm glad you could make it. Who are these ladies?" Axel asked.

"This is Sierra and Lyric. I thought they'd enjoy a night out."

"Very cool. Have you listened to our music before?" Axel asked us.

"Yes. We have. We can't wait to hear the songs live," Sierra said.

"We can't wait to play these songs live for you. By the way, this is my drummer, Tripp, and guitarist, Stryker." Axel pointed to two of his bandmates.

Both Tripp and Stryker had on all black, even down to their nail polish. They were both wearing black, baggy jeans with silver chains hooked all over them. Their shirts were black and long-sleeved but had different graphics of their band. They also wore thick black eyeliner, making their eyes, green and blue respectively, pop. They were interesting. I'd never seen anything like this band before.

"Hey, do you want to see who's opening for us?" Axel asked. "They're a kick-ass orchestra called Sacred Ethereal Symphony. Once we heard them, we knew they had to be our opening act."

"Of course. That would be so awesome," I said.

"I would definitely love that," Sierra chimed in.

We all followed Axel into a room filled with orchestral equipment. The players were sitting in their chairs in a semi-circle, waiting for the conductor to cue them in. Before the conductor could raise his baton to signal them to start, Axel yelled out to him, "Mr. Stewart, this is Lyric, Sierra, and Zane. They were invited to the concert tonight, and they got early-access passes to see our band, so I figured they would want to meet the orchestra too."

"Let's take five," Mr. Stewart said to the orchestra. He turned toward us. "Hello, my name is Charles, and I conduct this fine orchestra. I'm glad you could come out to see the band and us."

I scanned the whole room of orchestra members. They were also dressed in black. The men had on tuxedos, and the women wore dresses or skirts of some variety. My eyes landed on one woman who looked my age. She had long black hair and dark, almond-shaped eyes. She was breathtakingly beautiful. My heart skipped a beat. *Oh my God, there she is in the flesh.*

Sierra leaned in and whispered in my ear, "Are you okay?"

"Yeah. I'm fine. I'm fine," I said quietly, not wanting to take my eyes off the girl.

"Do you three have any questions for me?" Mr. Stewart asked us.

I wasn't really in the mood to ask him any questions. I was too busy focusing on this woman in front of me. But I didn't want her to know I was staring. So, every so often, I would look away and focus on something else. But her very existence kept drawing my eyes back to her spot in the room.

"What kind of music do you guys play?" Zane asked Charles.

"We play ethereal orchestral pieces. Most of the pieces were written by me." He looked proud.

"Oh, awesome. That's so cool," Sierra said. "Isn't it cool, Lyric?"

"Oh yeah, very cool," I said, not really paying attention.

"Well, thanks for stopping in to meet us. I'm sorry to cut this short, but we have to get back to practicing," Charles said.

"No problem. I look forward to seeing your guys' performance tonight," Sierra told him.

"Hopefully, you'll enjoy it and won't be disappointed."

"I'm sure you guys will be fantastic," I chimed in.

"Thank you for allowing these ladies to see what you guys do," Axel said.

"My pleasure," Charles said. He went back to conducting the orchestra.

Sierra, Zane, and I stood there for a little while longer to hear some of the piece they were playing. I looked directly at the girl as she played her violin. She was so focused on what she was playing, I didn't think she noticed me staring at her. Her black hair cascaded down her back. It looked so shiny and silky. I wanted to run my fingers through it. *Oh God, what am I thinking?* I needed to get out of this room as soon as possible.

"Ready?" Axel asked us.

"Yeah. We're ready," Sierra said.

The three of us followed Axel back to the lobby. Some fans recognized Axel and started to ask for pictures and autographs. He was nice enough to take a few pictures and sign some autographs. We stood off to the side and watched Axel in action. From the way he interacted with his fans, he seemed like a genuine and very humble guy, despite his gothic appearance.

"So, this is how the fans react to the band," Sierra asked Zane.

"Yes, and this is a smaller venue. Can you imagine a room full of thousands of adoring fans?" Zane asked.

"I can't imagine, can you, Lyric?" Sierra directed her question toward me.

"Umm . . . no," I said, not fully listening and staring into space.

I was still in my own little world, thinking about the black-haired girl. I couldn't believe she was in my dream. I hoped this wouldn't be the last time I saw her. But there was no way I could have spoken to her. Maybe I would be sent a miracle. I wanted to see her again, but in reality, the odds seemed slim to none.

"What did you think of the orchestra, Lyric?" Zane's question brought me back to the present.

I refocused on him. "Oh, they sounded awesome. I'm looking forward to hearing the other pieces they play tonight."

Sierra, Zane, and I made our way into the auditorium. After seeing both the orchestra and the band backstage, we were eager to be front and center. We wanted to experience everything that being in the front row had to offer. I sat next to Sierra, who seemed very eager to see Nightmarish Dreams. Zane sat on my other side. He barely said anything to me during the concert. I was glad. I didn't want to have to reiterate that I wasn't interested in him like that.

During the break between the orchestra and the band, Sierra asked me, "Are you sure you're okay? You've haven't been acting like yourself all night."

"I'm fine," I lied.

"You don't seem fine. You seem like you are in deep thought about something."

"I'm just trying to enjoy the concert, okay?" I snapped before realizing it.

"Well, I'm sorry if I'm disturbing you," Sierra said with the same energy.

The last thing I wanted to do is get defensive toward Sierra, but I was trying so hard to shove down these newfound feelings I had developed for this black-haired woman. While I watched her perform, I could sense her passion as a violinist. And for some reason, I wanted her to have that same passion for me. I was trying to figure out how I could see that woman again. I was drawn to her, and I wanted to see why. *Is it the way she plays the violin so beautifully? Is it the way she sways as she plays? It's like there is an unspoken dance between her and the violin.* For the life of me, I wasn't sure why I wanted to get to know her better. There was just something about her. *Dare I say a spiritual connection, even though we haven't communicated with each other . . . yet.* She consumed my thoughts for the rest of the concert.

"WANT to go get something to eat at Skyline Diner?" Zane asked Sierra and me after the concert.

"I don't know," I said. I wasn't up for eating at the diner. My mind was a jumbled mess, and all I wanted to do was sleep this off.

"Come on," Sierra insisted. "I'm starving."

I couldn't think straight, so I just agreed and followed along.

After we were sitting in a booth, I told Zane, "Thank you for inviting us to the concert."

"Oh, you're welcome. I hope you enjoyed it," he said.

"It was awesome. Both the band and the orchestra had a unique style. I loved them both. They really complemented each other." Warmth spread across my face and pooled in my stomach at the thought of how magnificent the beautiful woman had played.

"How about you, Sierra? What did you think?"

"I loved them. Like Lyric said, they complemented each other so well. I really enjoyed listening to them," Sierra answered while thumbing through the menu.

We talked a little more about the concert. My mind kept drifting back to the violinist. But I didn't want to bring up what I was thinking to Sierra or Zane. Frankly, it was none of their business. But a part of me wanted someone to talk to about what I was feeling. To figure out what those feelings were and what they meant, to reassure me that nothing was wrong with me. For now, I'd just have to journal. Journaling helped me sort out my feelings when I couldn't talk to anyone.

Sierra's foot connected lightly with my shin, jarring me from my thoughts. I glared at her, but she was watching Zane. Across the table, he was twisting his hands together. He seemed to resolve something, and his hands stilled. He looked at me.

"Lyric, umm . . . would you consider going out with me . . . alone?" Zane asked boldly.

Sierra's eyes got wide, and a smile formed on her lips. I knew she'd been waiting for this moment the whole night. After Zane had left Sierra's tattoo shop the day we met him, she'd told me that he was handsome and creatively dressed. Since I was also a dancer, she thought he would match my energy and possibly bring a new self-awareness to our different genres of dance. But I was so torn. Going out with Zane wasn't going to help sort out what I was feeling in my heart for this violinist, however confusing it was.

"Zane, I'm going to have to decline your offer. I'm just going through a really weird phase at the moment. I'd rather not rush into dating right now," I told him honestly.

"Uhh . . . okay," Zane said.

"I'm sorry. I hope you understand. You seem like a nice guy. It's just, right now is not the right time."

Sierra sat there with her jaw on the floor. I knew she didn't think I would blatantly turn down Zane right in front of her. But she also didn't know about the inner struggle I was going through ever since I saw the beautiful violinist.

The rest of the time at the diner was somewhat awkward. We tried to play it off, but there was tension between us. When our food came, we ate quickly. After we were done, we thanked Zane, and then Sierra and I left the diner.

CHAPTER 4

Xenia

One week after my orchestra's performance and the Nightmarish Dreams concert at the convention center, my family and I were headed back there again. This time to see Mei perform with her Rhythm in Motion Dance Troupe. I was so grateful that my family had seen my performance. It had been comforting to have family there and know they supported me. Plus, they'd been excited to see me perform. Now I was equally excited to support Mei by being at her performance.

It had been awhile since I'd seen Mei in her element. She lived and breathed dance. If any profession was made for her, it was certainly dance. I remembered the first time I'd seen Mei perform. She'd been so graceful and fluid in her movements, it had taken my breath away. The admiration I had for dancers grew tremendously after I saw Mei perform that first time.

I had told my mom, Aunt Tao, and Mei that I would meet them at the convention center. I had to clean my apartment. After my orchestra practices for the concert we just had, I had been just too exhausted to do anything more than the bare necessities. Mostly I came home and crashed. But now that the performance was over and practices had resumed a normal schedule, I could finally take some time to really clean.

I was still lying in bed after waking up, so I climbed out and hopped in the shower. I would probably have to take another shower after I finished cleaning, but I didn't really care. After my quick shower, I threw on some old sweats and put my hair in a high messy bun. The first area I was going to tackle was my kitchen, and all my dishes were piled up in the sink. Looking back now, it would have been easier to wash a plate and silverware each night rather than having to wash all my dishes at once.

After I finished with the kitchen, I inspected the living room, which wasn't too bad. It just needed a good vacuuming. So I quickly vacuumed my living room and straightened the pillows on the couch. Then I checked the time to make sure I could finish the majority of my cleaning before Mei's dance performance.

The dance performance started at 2 p.m., which was in an hour, so I decided to finish cleaning afterward. I opted to take another shower because I was a little sweaty. After my shower, I picked out an outfit to wear—dark-wash jeans, a white blouse with black pinstripes, and black loafers. I wore my hair down and finger-waved it.

The drive to the venue wasn't as bad as I thought. The traffic was light for one thirty on a Saturday afternoon. I got to the venue in no time at all, parked my car, and walked inside the building to search for my mom and Aunt Tao. A few moments later, I spotted them sitting on a long plush bench in the lobby. I walked up to them.

"Xen, what took you so long?" my mom asked with a little frown.

"I told you I had to straighten up my apartment first. I'm actually not that late," I said.

"I know your apartment couldn't have been that messy," she complained.

I sighed. It didn't matter what I said. She would be disappointed no matter what. So I quit while I was ahead. I turned my attention to Aunt Tao instead. "So, Aunt Tao, are you excited to see Mei perform?" I asked.

"I'm so excited. We better get in there to find seats close enough," she said.

"Yes, we better," my mom said as she rolled her eyes at me.

We made our way into the auditorium and sat toward the front. Just one week before, I had been in the pit performing with the orchestra as the opening act for Nightmarish Dreams. It was different now that I was in the audience about to watch Mei dance. I could only imagine how nervous she must be. I had been so nervous myself and had just wanted to get my notes right. I hadn't wanted to be the one to mess up the orchestra's entire performance. Thankfully it had all worked out in the end. We'd been praised by the audience as well as the band. So whatever nerves Mei had, I was sure they would quickly melt away once she was on stage with her fellow dancers.

My mom, Aunt Tao, and I each thumbed through the programs we were given. Surprisingly, there were no pictures of the dance troupe on the program, only names and bios. I thought it was weird, but I didn't make the programs. After a few minutes, the lights began to flicker, signaling that the performance was about to start.

I looked over at my mom and Aunt Tao, who both had huge grins on their faces. They each had their cell phones on camera mode, ready to take pictures. I was excited to see Mei dance again. I wasn't that worried about taking pictures. I just wanted to be in the moment, watching the performance in real time.

Soon the dancers entered the stage. They each took their places and froze in a different pose, waiting for the music. When the music started, it was an up-tempo song. Each dancer's movements matched the beat of the song. Mei danced like her life depended on it; she was on fire. I yelled her name at one point during the performance. She most likely didn't hear my lone scream among the various claps and noises the crowd was making. But it felt good to think she heard it.

I scanned the stage, observing the dancers. They were all moving in time to the beat and all in sync with one another. As I was focusing on the other dancers, one of the girls caught my eye. She looked about my height and wore a really pretty costume. Even though they were all wearing the same costumes, it looked especially good on her. Her sandy-brown hair was pulled into a high bun. I couldn't take my eyes off her. She was beautiful. My heart started racing, and it felt like she took the air right out of my lungs. Goosebumps formed underneath my skin. *I can't breathe.* I started to hyperventilate and felt my cheeks flush. *You don't like girls, Xenia. What is going on with you?* I couldn't figure out why just staring at her evoked such strong emotions in me.

I kept sitting there, trying to stay calm, watching the performance. But after a few more minutes, my heart was still racing, and I could feel my cheeks flushing. *Well, this is new. Okay, don't freak out*, I thought. I wasn't sure what to make of this newfound desire, but at that same time, I was taken aback. I looked at both my mom and Aunt Tao, their eyes glued on Mei. I was glad because I didn't want them to see me staring at the other dancer. I was sweating profusely. *I hope they don't see me sweating like this.* When my mom glanced over my way for a brief second, I quickly grabbed the program and pretended I was looking through it. *That was a close call.*

For the rest of the performance, my eyes darted between Mei and the other dancer. There was something intriguing about her. I wanted to get to know her and what she was all about. But I would have to be cautious how I went about it. My mom and Aunt Tao couldn't find out I liked this woman yet. The final dance the group performed was a ballad to a slower tempo. It was so moving. I was in awe.

After the performance, the three of us went to the lobby. We waited on the plush bench for Mei to come out so we could congratulate her. As I was sitting there, my thoughts kept returning to the other dancer. I felt my cheeks getting flushed again and heat rising in my body. I put my head in my hands. *Why is this girl consuming my mind like this?* I was still lost in thought when my mom and Aunt Tao's quiet conversation became loud and excited. I looked up. Mei had finally come out wearing sweats. Her hair was in a ponytail, and she held her dance bag.

"Congratulations, Mei, you danced beautifully," Aunt Tao gushed as she gave her daughter a huge hug.

"You were wonderful," my mom echoed Aunt Tao's sentiments.

"I really enjoyed seeing you dance again, Mei," I said.

"Thank you. I'm so glad you all came to see me dance. I'm so grateful," Mei stated.

We stood there and talked about the performance a little more. Then Mei motioned for someone to come over. It was the woman I had been staring at during the performance. Her hair was still in that bun and she was also wearing sweats. Fly-away pieces of hair swept across her forehead as she smoothed them down with her fingers. It made me wonder what else her fingers could do. The way her sweats hugged her curves left me imagining her wearing nothing but her birthday suit.

"Hey, everyone, this is Lyric. She's an incredible dancer, and I want you to meet her," Mei said.

"Hi. It's nice to meet you," Lyric said, smiling.

"It's nice to meet one of the dancers that Mei gets to practice with on a regular basis," Aunt Tao said happily.

Lyric stared at me with a puzzled look on her face. It almost seemed like she was trying to make out where she knew me from, but I had never seen her before today.

"Lyric, we are planning to go to Café Ciel after we leave here. Would you like to join us?" Mei asked Lyric, breaking her stare.

I hope she says yes, I thought. *I want to get to know her.* I waited for her to answer.

"Sure, I would love to join you guys," she said. "I'm just going to call my roommate and update her on what I'm doing." She took out her phone and stepped off to the side.

I watched her talking to her roommate. I couldn't make out what Lyric was saying, but I was entranced. I couldn't take my eyes off her. As soon as Lyric ended her phone call, she made her way back over to us.

"All good?" Mei asked.

"Yes. My roommate, Sierra, worries if I don't show up at home when I say I will. We have each other's backs like that," Lyric explained.

"Awesome. Well, let's go then," Mei said.

WHEN WE HAD all arrived at the café in our respective cars, we walked in together, grabbed the nearest table, and sat down.

"This is the first time I've been to this café. It's quite cozy and cute," Lyric said, looking around.

"We come here quite often. The avocado toast is so good," Mei said.

The server came and handed us the menus.

"Oh. The avocado toast does look good," Lyric said as she was looking through the menu.

After we ordered, Aunt Tao and Mom went to use the restroom. This left just Lyric, Mei, and I sitting at the table. I wanted to ask Lyric some questions, but I didn't know exactly what I wanted to ask.

Lyric beat me to it. "So, Xenia, what do you do?"

"I play the violin in an orchestra." I started to unwrap the napkin from around my silverware.

"Oh, that's so cool. I recently saw a fantastic orchestra. I loved hearing them perform." Xenia also started unwrapping her napkin from around her silverware.

"That's awesome. Yeah, playing in the orchestra was something I was born to do."

"Kind of like me with dance. I couldn't imagine not ever dancing," Lyric said.

"Me either. Dance is my life," Mei chimed in.

We talked a little more about how we chose our career paths. I listened intently to Lyric expressively talk about why she'd chosen dance over going to college. At first, her parents had been a little leery that she'd wanted to be a professional dancer. But when they'd seen how serious Lyric was, her parents had eventually warmed up to the idea of her dancing professionally.

I couldn't stop staring at Lyric's lips. They were lush and full. I couldn't help feeling like I wanted to kiss them. Soon, my mom and Aunt Tao came back to the table. They broke my eyes away from staring at Lyric's lips while Mei filled them

43

in on what we were discussing while they were in the restroom.

A few moments later, the server came with our drinks and food. As we ate, we discussed the dance performance.

"I'm going to use the restroom," Lyric said during a break in our conversation.

She got up and headed toward the restroom, while Mei, Aunt Tao and my mom continued to talk. I watched Lyric walk to the restroom. The opportunity to talk to her one-on-one was now. So I also excused myself and went to the restroom.

When I entered the restroom, I stood waiting for Lyric to come out of the stall. I knew this was some small type of stalk-erish shit, but I didn't really care. I wanted to talk to Lyric alone without the eyes of Mei, Aunt Tao, and Mom. My mind was spinning with all the questions I wanted to ask her. Soon Lyric stepped out of the stall. She looked up at me and seemed kind of surprised I was standing in front of her.

"Hi," Lyric said, her head cocked to the side.

"I know this looks crazy, but I wanted to ask you something," I said.

"Umm . . . okay." She went to the sink to wash her hands.

"The orchestra you went to see, were they opening for a band named Nightmarish Dreams?"

As Lyric continued to wash her hands, she looked toward me, and her eyes lit up. "Yes. As a matter of fact, they were."

"The reason I asked that is because I'm in that orchestra," I said.

"Oh . . . really? You guys were amazing," she gushed.

"Thank you so much for the compliment."

"You're welcome." Her cheeks blushed a little.

Lyric dried her hands with a paper towel, and I saw her smile to herself. It was the most perfect smile I'd ever seen.

Even in these few moments alone together in this restroom, I wanted to spend more time alone with her. Even though I only asked her about the concert she saw, I felt a connection. I couldn't believe Lyric saw me in concert performing with the orchestra. *What a small world.*

After Lyric finished drying her hands, we exited the restroom and walked back to the table to finish eating.

"What took you girls so long?" Mei questioned.

Lyric and I looked at one another and smiled.

"Oh nothing. It was just that we got to talking for a bit," I said.

Mei, my mom, and Aunt Tao looked at each other then looked at us as we sat down, but no one said a word.

After we were all finished eating, we sat there in silence for a few moments.

"It was really nice to meet you, Lyric," my mom said after a while.

"Thank you for inviting me. It was nice getting to know Mei's family," Lyric said.

"We were glad you came along," Aunt Tao added.

"I hope we made you feel welcomed," Mei said.

"Yes, you all did. Thank you." Lyric looked down at her hands and folded them together. It was like she didn't want to make eye contact with me. *I guess I get it.* The brief interaction we had in the bathroom probably threw her for a loop, finding out who I was. But I needed and wanted to know what was going through her mind.

"I'm glad to have gotten to know you a little bit, Lyric. You're a phenomenal dancer. I'm glad you are Mei's friend," I said.

"It was nice to meet you too," Lyric said. She started to stand from the table, while seemingly avoiding my gaze. "Thank you again for a lovely time."

"It was our pleasure," my mom said.

"I'll see you in class, Mei." Lyric started walking to the door.

"See you in class," Mei said. "Drive home safely."

Lyric turned and waved to us as she stepped out of the café. I just sat there. *Who did I just meet and how can I meet up with her again?*

CHAPTER 5

Lyric

"Sierra, I'm back," I yelled as I came through the front door of our apartment.

"I'm in the living room. Now get in here. I want to hear all about how your performance went," Sierra said.

I hurried to my room to put my dance bag down and quickly change into my pajamas. I stepped into the living room to find Sierra curled up in a blanket. She was watching some kind of reality show on TV.

"Took you long enough," she said.

"I wanted to get comfortable." I sat beside her on the couch, pulling my legs up under me.

"So, tell me about your performance." Sierra turned toward me and gave me her undivided attention.

"It was magical. I danced like I never danced before. The crowd went wild for us," I gushed.

"That's awesome. I'm sorry I couldn't be there to see you dance." Sierra slouched back down.

I could sense her disappointment about not be able to come to my performance.

"It's okay. I know how busy you are with work and all," I said.

"So where did you go afterward?"

"Oh, I was invited to a café with a fellow dancer and her family." I shifted on the couch.

"And how did that go?"

I had to hold back the huge grin I wanted to show her. Meeting Xenia was the definite highlight of being invited to go with them. Not to mention, finding out she was the girl I had been crushing on at the concert. My mind was blown. I decided to ease into this conversation with Sierra.

"It went very well," I said as a smile formed on my lips.

"What? Why are you smiling like that?"

"Well . . . umm . . . do you remember that concert we went to?" I asked.

"Yes. What about it?"

"I met the girl that was in the orchestra at the concert that night."

"What girl?" Sierra looked puzzled.

Oh shit. I forgot I didn't tell Sierra about the girl I was crushing on at the concert. I guess I need to come clean about what I am feeling for this girl. My mind was jumbled, and I couldn't think straight. My mouth was dry. Trying to form the words to express what I wanted to say was proving difficult. I took a deep breath. "Do you remember when Zane took us backstage to meet the orchestra?"

"Yes . . ."

"Well, there was a girl . . . I . . . umm . . . was crushing on a little bit," I confessed.

"Oh . . ." Sierra's raised her eyebrow.

"I found out this afternoon that her name is Xenia, and she's the cousin of a girl I dance with."

"Is this the reason you turned down Zane at the diner?" Sierra asked.

"Maybe . . . I don't know. I'm still trying to process it myself."

"But I thought you were into guys?" Sierra said, waiting for me to answer.

"That's what I thought too. But I'm so attracted to this girl," I said, turning to face her.

"Maybe if you gave Zane a chance, you know?" Sierra said.

"Zane is attractive, don't get me wrong. But I'm just not attracted to him in *that* way." I quickly zeroed my attention back to the TV show.

"You mean sexually?" She grabbed me and turned me back to face her.

I stared at her. I blinked multiple times and swallowed hard. Again, the words escaped me. I looked around the room, at anything but Sierra. I didn't want to look into her eyes when I told her that I was sexually attracted to this woman.

"Yes," I said to the rug.

"So, you really like this girl." Sierra turned down the volume of the TV.

"I do. I really do. But I don't know if she's into girls or would even be willing to give me a chance," I told Sierra honestly.

"I see. Maybe you could ask her cousin about her," Sierra said as she headed to the kitchen to get something to drink.

She came back into the living room with two glasses of wine.

Taking one of the glasses from her hand and took a sip. "I don't know if I would have the courage to ask. I'm afraid that she isn't into girls and that would devastate me."

"But you'll never know unless you ask, Lyric." She sipped on her wine.

"That's true." I thought about Sierra's statement. "Maybe I'll ask Mei about Xenia at the next practice."

"That's the spirit. I'm sure everything will go fine," Sierra said reassuringly.

I sighed. "Hopefully."

Sierra picked up the remote and started tiredly flipping through the channels to find something else to watch since the reality show had ended. "Ugh . . . nothing else is on," she complained.

"It's alright. I'll think I'll go to bed. I'm tired; it's been a long day. Thank you for listening to me about my crush and not judging me."

"No problem. You know you can talk to me about anything, right?"

"I know," I said. "Good night."

"Good night, Lyric."

I got up off the couch and ventured to my room. I wanted to write about my experience this afternoon. So, I grabbed my journal and a pen off my nightstand. Sitting on my bed, I began writing. I wrote and wrote, pouring my heart, soul, and even some tears on the paper. I felt relieved to be able to fully express myself, things I couldn't even tell Sierra. After I finished, I closed my journal and put in it my nightstand drawer. I climbed under my various blankets and closed my eyes. I was so close to drifting off to sleep when my cell vibrated.

> Mom: Lyric, I'm sorry your father and I missed your dance performance. You know how busy we are with work. But we miss you. Could you come over tomorrow? We'd like to catch up and hear all about your performance. Love you.

Both my mom and dad work in the entertainment industry. My mom, Vada, is a makeup artist, and my dad, Sage, is a producer. So, they both have been busy working on TV and film sets. They both knew how this business was, so when I told them I wanted to be a professional dancer, they'd been hesitant. They'd wanted me to have a college degree to fall back on. But I didn't really want to do anything but dance. They'd enrolled me in a dance school as soon as I was a freshman in high school. I knew that was late given some dancers danced all their lives. When I was little, my friends and I had made up dances and put on shows for the neighborhood parents and kids. That was when I'd known I'd wanted to make dance a priority in my life.

I quickly texted my mom back.

> Me: I will visit you guys tomorrow. Have a great night. I love you.

After I sent the message, I started to grow anxious, my stomach turning in knots. My parents were very adamant about wanting me to get married. I dreaded the fact that at some point during our conversation, the subject of marriage would come up, and I wasn't ready. I didn't want to tell them about my new crush yet. They were always hounding me about getting married. Which was totally understandable. But a part of me didn't want to let them down because it just wasn't the case anymore that I'd be marrying a man. I had a new option I was willing to explore. I thought they would be supportive given the industry they were in but was really hard to tell. I put my phone back down on my nightstand and readjusted in my blankets. I drifted off to sleep as soon as I closed my eyes.

I SLEPT in and woke up with the mindset that whatever happened, happened. I couldn't worry about it any longer. I lay in my bed for a few minutes to fully wake up. I thought about the most random things, like what I would wear to meet my parents. It wasn't really a big deal; I could wear anything to meet them. But my focus was still on trying to control this outcome. I just needed to take a deep breath in, exhale, and relax. I did this a few times until I felt myself calm down.

After a few more minutes, I decided to get up and start the day. I quickly hopped in the shower and washed my hair. I wanted to try a different look, so I opted to wear it curly. I brushed my teeth and then applied Cantu's curly cream generously throughout my damp sandy-brown hair. Then I blow-dried my hair with a diffuser to try and fluff up the curls, which took a while because my hair was so long. When I was done, I went back into my room and fished out a pair of my light denim jeans and a casual black top. I checked myself out in the full-length mirror hanging on my closet door. Approving, I went to the kitchen to figure out what to make myself for breakfast.

Sierra was at the table, eating cereal. "Good morning. You slept late. It's almost noon."

"Same for you I see. Good morning." I took out the blender, fruit, and almond milk. I threw all the ingredients inside the blender and turned it on. After it was blended, I poured the smoothie in a tall glass and joined Sierra at the table. "So, what are your plans for today?" I asked, taking a sip of my smoothie.

"It's my day off so nothing really. You?" She took a bite of cereal.

"Lucky you. I have to go visit my parents today, which I don't mind, but I'm also terrified because they always ask me when I'm going to get married or if I met a guy yet."

"Oh, I see. You don't know how your parents would take it if they found out you like girls?"

"Exactly."

"Well, don't tell them then. It's not a hard and fast rule that you have to tell them. You tell them when you are ready," Sierra finished her last bite of cereal and proceeded to drink the milk out of the bowl.

"That's so true. I don't have to tell my parents," I repeated. "I can tell them on my own terms. Thanks, Sierra."

"No problem. That's what I'm here for, to listen and give advice. Did your parents give you a time to come over?"

"No. They didn't. But I guess I'll head over there soon. So, just relaxing for the day?" I finished up my smoothie.

"Yep, I mean, I will most likely free draw some tattoo ideas for my clients, probably take a nap, and possibly hang with Everly," Sierra said.

"Oh, that sounds like a relaxing but productive day." Sierra and I talked a little more about her plans. After a few minutes, I said, "Well, I think I'm going to go now."

"Okay. Good luck, and remember what I told you," Sierra said reassuringly.

"I will. Thanks again." I got up from the table. I grabbed my sling bag and car keys from my room. "Bye, Sierra," I said as I walked out the front door to my car.

THE DRIVE TO MY PARENTS' house took fifteen minutes. I was in my thoughts the entire time. Overthinking was the worst, but I remembered what Sierra told me. *I don't have to say anything about Xenia. I can tell them on my terms.* This settled my nerves tremendously.

A little before one o'clock, I parked my car behind my dad's car, got out, and walked up the driveway. I rang the doorbell and waited for what seemed like eternity. *It doesn't usually take them this long to answer the door. They must be on a business call or something.* Finally, the door flung open. There stood my mom in a designer suit with her hair down and makeup on point.

"Hey, baby girl, I'm sorry I had you waiting. Your dad and I were talking to potential clients." She embraced me.

"It's okay. I wasn't waiting that long." I hugged her back.

"Come in. We want to hear all about your dance performance," my mom said excitedly.

I stepped inside. My parents' house was a miniature version of the houses on MTV cribs. They had marble floors and high ceilings. Their couch was black leather. My parents definitely worked hard to afford what they have. This hardworking mindset had spilled over to me. When I'd decided to pursue a career in dance, I'd set a rigorous workout and practice schedule right from the start. I got up for early mornings and had late nights. I was determined that I was going to work my ass off to achieve my dream.

"Hey, Dad," I said as I entered the living room.

"How's my favorite dancer?" He stood up, walked over to me, gave me a hug, and then sat back down.

"I'm good, Dad. How have you been?"

"Busy, baby girl. We might start working with this cast on a new reality TV show." He sat on the love seat, typing away on his laptop.

"Oh . . . that's great, Dad." I sat on the leather couch.

"Do you want any water, soda, or wine, sweetheart?" my mom asked.

"Wine, please."

Even though the subject of guys and marriage hadn't even been brought up yet, I was still overthinking. I need something to relax me and give me a little buzz. My mom poured two glasses of white wine from the bar and walked over and handed it to me.

"So . . ." Holding her wine glass, she took a seat beside my dad.

"The performance, it was so good. We had a large crowd in the audience. They went wild for us." I sipped my wine.

"That's great. I'm so sorry we missed it, Lyric."

"When is your next performance?" my dad asked. "Your mom and I will make sure our scheduled are cleared, so we can come to see you dance."

"I don't know yet. But when I do, I will let you know," I told them.

"Okay. Did you meet any guys yet? You know, you aren't getting any younger," my dad said.

There it was—the dreaded question. I took another sip of wine before I answered him. "Well, Dad, I'm twenty-five not thirty-five. I have plenty of time to be in a relationship and get married. I'm just focusing on my dancing career right now." I took another sip of my wine.

"Honey, you can't dance forever," my mom chimed in. "Your father and I want you to experience love and happiness like we have."

"I know. Your relationship is something I look up to. I'm

just not ready for one right now. But when I am, you guys will be the first to know," I said trying to reassure them.

"Okay . . . okay. We won't push the subject anymore. Your mother and I were just curious, that's all," my dad said.

I let my head fall back on the couch and let out a long sigh. It was a weight lifted off my shoulders that we didn't have to talk about the topic more. Now I could finally relax. "Can I have another small glass of wine?" I asked my mom.

"Aren't you driving?" she asked.

"Yes. But I'll be okay. Another small glass won't hurt."

My mom took my glass and refilled it. She came back and handed me the glass. It was only filled a quarter of the way.

I looked at the glass. "Really, Mom?"

"I'd rather you be safe than sorry, sweetheart." She sat beside Dad again.

"So, how's Sierra doing?" he asked.

"Oh, she's doing well. Her business is thriving."

"By the way, there are some young guys and girls on this new show we might be working on, and when we met with some of them, we overheard them talking about wanting to get tattoos. Of course, the first person we thought about was Sierra."

"Oh. Well, if you could get their contact information, I could pass it on to Sierra. She should be able to set them up with appointments sometime," I said.

"Good to know, I will definitely get back to you."

The rest of the afternoon, my parents and I talked about their upcoming projects. We also reminisced about how they started out in the entertainment industry. It was a chill day, and for that I was glad. I had been all worked up for nothing. *When I do tell them about Xenia, the time will be right.*

CHAPTER 6

Xenia

I was late to orchestra practice, which was a first for me. I slipped in quickly, sitting in my chair among the first violins. Mr. Charles looked straight at me with disapproval from the podium. I quickly shot my eyes downward to my sheet music. He then went back to conducting the orchestra. I knew I would hear about this later, so I mentally prepared myself. If I was honest, my head had been in the clouds thinking about Lyric. I was so focused on how I could see her again. But that was no excuse for being late to practice. I needed something better to tell him when he asked. I'd have to come up with something soon. I didn't like lying, but considering I wasn't ready to even tell my parents what was going on, I had no choice.

My mind was definitely not at practice tonight. I missed a few notes and even lost my place once while I was playing. It was so unlike me. *This girl really has a hold on me, but this isn't a good time. Concentrate, don't be distracted*, I kept telling myself. Mr. Charles looked at me multiple times throughout practice. He was probably wondering what the hell was going on. All I could do was give him a half smile.

After practice was finished, sure enough, Mr. Charles called me over. "Xenia, you are one of my best violinists. You were off tonight. Is something wrong?"

"I'm just under some stress right now, that's all. I'm sorry I was late," I said.

"Is this getting to be too much for you? Because if it is . . . you have my permission to take a short break. You can come back when you are ready to play again," Mr. Charles said.

"No . . . it's not. I promise I'll be better next practice," I said, hoping he wouldn't push a break on me.

"That's good to hear. But if you're not playing better by the next practice, I'll have no choice but to put you on a temporary break. You understand?"

"Yes, I do." I pressed my lips together as I lowered my head. Tears were trying to well up, but when I looked back up, I gave Mr. Charles a curt nod. I needed to get my priorities straight. Being a violinist in this orchestra was the priority right now; it paid my bills. I would have to snap the fuck out of whatever this was, because my job was on the line.

I started packing up my violin and songbook. Out of the corner of my eye, I saw Brielle watching me. After a couple of seconds, I still felt her gaze, so I looked up at her.

"Are you okay? You were kind of off tonight," she said.

"Yeah, I'm fine. Just a little stressed at the moment," I told her.

"What did Mr. Charles want?"

"Just to have a little talk about how I performed tonight."

"Oh, I see. Well, if you want to talk about it, I'm here."

"I appreciate that, Bri. But I'm okay."

"If you change your mind . . ." She trailed off.

I just nodded, continuing to pack up my things. I needed to get out of here before I took Bri up on her offer and spilled my heart to her. I wasn't ready to let someone else know how

I felt about Lyric yet. "I'll see you at the next practice." I stood up and swung my bag over my shoulder and picked up my violin.

"Okay." Brielle gave me a wry smile.

I hated to leave Bri in the dark about what I was going through. She was a good friend, but I didn't know how she would take my confession of liking a girl. I didn't want any negativity. I was trying to keep as positive as I could. Even though I didn't know the next time I would see Lyric.

I waved to the group as I left the practice area and stepped outside. It was raining. Not knowing it was going to rain, I hadn't brought my umbrella, so I briskly walked to my car and climbed in. I turned the radio on a low volume just to have some background noise. I was determined to drown out my thoughts as I drove home. *I can't believe this girl is consuming my mind like this. I really need ask Mei about her. Yes, I'm scared to even mention it to her, but I will never know if I don't ask.*

I FINALLY REACHED MY APARTMENT, unlocked my front door, and ventured inside. I placed my violin and songbook near the door and plopped down on the couch. I sat there contemplating whether I should text Mei to come over. Her husband was likely still at work, so it should be a good time to come over and chat. I texted her.

> Me: Mei, are you busy? Can you come over? I need to talk to you about something.

> Mei: No, I'm not busy. I can swing by. Is everything okay?

> Me: Yes, yes. I didn't mean to alarm you. I'll fill you in when you get here.

> Mei: Great, see you soon.

I stared at our messages, then set my phone down. *I can't believe I'm going to really go through with this. I'm going to tell Mei the truth about my feelings for Lyric. I am so nervous, but I can do this.* I took a few deep breaths—in and out, in and out. *Whatever the outcome of our conversation will be, I'm ready to accept it. But that won't change the way I feel about Lyric, even if Mei disapproves. Hopefully she doesn't. But it's not every day your cousin tells you she likes girls after previously solely liking guys.*

I straightened up the living room a bit before Mei arrived and grabbed myself a quick bite to eat. I hadn't really eaten anything before orchestra practice. *Damn, Lyric is so embedded in my brain, I'm forgetting to eat. I have to get a handle on this shit before I can't do anything other than think of her.* I sighed. All I wanted to do was think about her, but it wasn't looking good for my career. I was already on Mr. Charles's radar, and there was no need to make it any worse.

I quickly ate the turkey-and-cheese sandwich I made, chugging a glass of water behind it. Water was not my first choice, but I didn't think being inebriated while talking to Mei about Lyric would help my case. I sat on the couch and flipped aimlessly through the TV channels to pass the time while I waited for Mei. My palms were sweaty, so sweaty that I almost dropped the remote. As I was making my way through the endless array of channels, there was a knock on my door, finally.

When I opened the door, there stood Mei. She was wearing a pair of black sweatpants and a black hoodie.

"Hey, I got here as fast as I could," Mei said. She came in and sat on the couch.

"I told you it wasn't urgent."

"Oh, whatever. So, what's up?"

I sat beside Mei, taking an inward breath.

She looked at me, patient and calm.

"I like Lyric. I mean . . . I *like her* like her," I blurted out.

It took a couple of seconds for Mei to register what I just confessed to her. As soon as she comprehended what I said, her eyes went wide. "You *like her* like her? As in more than a friendly way?"

"Yes, I do."

"Umm . . . I don't know what to say. You know this won't go down well with our family."

"I wasn't planning on—"

"Telling them?" she finished the thought for me. "You know where that got me, Xenia. I couldn't keep the family from the fact that I was dating Qiang because they would have still planned my wedding to some other man. Where would that have gotten me?"

"But Qiang is a guy. So even though they didn't choose him for you, once they saw you truly loved him and he loved you, it was easier to accept him into the family."

"Yeah. That's the one advantage. Qiang is a guy, and my parents saw that he was hard-working, loyal, and caring. These were all the qualities they wanted in the husband for me. If they didn't see those qualities in him, I probably would be married to the man they had for me. But I'm grateful my parents warmed up to Qiang when I told them I was dating him."

"I supported you when they questioned if Qiang would be a good match for you, remember that?" I explained.

"Yes, I do. But what do you want me to do? I can't magically make your parents accept who you like," Mei said honestly.

"I know that. But you could vouch for me when I decide to tell them."

"Like that will go over well." She leaned back and rested her head against the back of the couch. "Lyric is a woman. For all you know, if you two did decide to date, what makes you think it would be genuine? She could just be using you for experimental purposes. Have you ever thought about that? And her being Black? Our family isn't racist, but keeping our culture and traditions intact is very important."

"For experimental purposes?" *How could she even think that?* "No, I don't think she would experiment with me. And what does her being Black have anything to do with keeping our culture and traditions? We can still incorporate Chinese culture and traditions as a same-sex couple," I reasoned.

I couldn't believe Mei right now. After all I did to support her and Qiang, she had the nerve to downplay my feelings for Lyric. Saying I would be an experiment if Lyric and I got together? *How dare she.* I have the same right as she did to be in love with someone who would love me back and not have it be one-sided. But since Lyric wasn't a guy, she didn't see it that way.

"Why don't you make it easy on yourself and just get engaged to Jun Lee like everyone is expecting," she said.

"Because I don't know him, Mei. Nor do I care to get to know him," I said defensively.

"Well, you don't know Lyric either." Mei also sounded defensive.

"My point is I want to get to know her."

Mei just shook her head. She knew me well enough to know she wouldn't be able to change how I felt about Lyric.

I felt alone. I knew there was a possibility that this conversation would go south. But I thought since Mei had faced disapproval in the beginning with Qiang, she would have some sympathy for me and my situation.

"Hey, I'm sorry to up and run out on you, but Qiang will be home soon," Mei said as she checked the time on her phone.

"It's okay. I understand. Wifely duties calling," I replied, trying to sound humorous. I was upset, but I didn't want us to part on bad terms.

"Maybe you'll know soon enough too."

I wasn't sure if I wanted to *know*. I liked my life. Playing with the orchestra, living on my own. Sure, I wanted a relationship . . . companionship . . . just not with Jun Lee. Even though I wasn't sure if I'd have a choice, I did know that I'd rather spend a little time with Lyric before I had to marry some strange man than spend no time with her at all. It wasn't the time to ask Mei if she knew how I could contact Lyric. But I secretly wished that Lyric was thinking the same thing about wanting to get to know me and would contact me.

"Just remember what I said. Make it easy on yourself, Xenia." Mei stood to get ready to leave and pulled me in for a hug.

I reluctantly hugged her back. I knew she meant well by wanting me to experience as little heartache as possible. But what if her parents hadn't accepted Qiang and she'd had no choice but to marry the man they'd chosen for her? Mei would be singing a different tune right now. I just had to do what was right for me.

After Mei left, I sat on the couch going over the conversation we just had in my mind. I had supported her dating Qiang from the beginning, even when her parents had questions about his abilities to care and love her. This wasn't the

1900s; it wasn't right for them to choose who we married. But I had stood by Mei, despite their apprehensions in the beginning. Her refusal to stand by me now really hurt. *I really don't want to be alone in this*, I thought. I really wanted someone in my corner. I thought about calling Brielle and running my situation by her. I didn't feel like Brielle would judge me, but there was only one way to find out.

I picked up my phone and scrolled down my contact list until I found Brielle's name. I started to push the call button but suddenly hesitated. *You can do this*, I told myself. I counted to three, took a deep breath in, exhaled out, and hit the call button. As it started to ring, I started to panic. Thankfully, Brielle answered after it rang twice.

"Hi, Xenia," Brielle said.

"Hey, Bri. Sorry to call you so late, but I need to talk to somebody."

"It's okay. Is everything alright?" she asked.

"Umm . . . not really. My cousin Mei and I had a conversation tonight, and she told me she had reservations about who I like."

"Who wouldn't like the guy you like? I'm sure he's a real gentleman," she said.

"The *girl* I like," I corrected her.

"Girl? Oh . . . the girl you like. You like girls? No judgment here. You know I love you and will support you no matter what," Brielle said reassuringly.

I sank into the couch with relief. "Yes, I do. And thank you, I needed that. My cousin said she wouldn't support or vouch for me when I told my parents," I said.

"I see. That's a shame. Does the girl know you like her? What's her name?"

"Her name is Lyric, and not quite. I was planning to ask

Mei how to get in contact with her. But after Mei blatantly refused to vouch or support me, I didn't bother asking her."

"Okay. Well, is there any way you can get her number?"

"I'm afraid Mei was the only way I had," I stated.

"I'm a big believer in what's supposed to happen will happen, no matter what," Brielle said.

"Thank you, I needed that reassurance."

"You're welcome. That's what friends are for," Brielle said.

I was so happy that Brielle didn't judge me for liking girls. I was so worried that I would have no support on this matter. It was a relief. Even if I didn't have Mei's support, I had Brielle's, and that would be enough.

"Hey, it's late, I don't want to keep you on the phone forever. Thank you for listening and supporting me, Bri," I said.

"No problem. If you ever need to talk to someone, I'm always here to listen. I'll talk to you later. Have a great night."

"You too, Bri. Bye." I ended the call.

This night had turned out much better than the way it had started. I went to my room, threw on my pajamas, and climbed into my bed. I started thinking through the conversations I had with Mei and Brielle. I thought about both of their reactions as well as the fears and hopes I had about being with Lyric in the future. It must have been a relief to my heart to think about the whole situation because the next thing I knew, my alarm was going off, and it was morning.

CHAPTER 7
Lyric

All morning, I thought about how I would ask Mei about Xenia. It would be easier to ask Mei about Xenia if I was asking to be Xenia's friend. But that wasn't the case, so I was hella nervous about what Mei would think once I asked for Xenia's number. *Maybe I am over-thinking it. Maybe Mei won't think anything of it*, I told myself. Dance practice wasn't until this afternoon, so I had some time to come up with a way of asking Mei about her cousin.

I threw on some lounge clothes and went to the kitchen to grab something for breakfast. Today I was in the mood for pancakes. I grabbed two frozen pancakes out of the freezer and put them in the toaster. While the pancakes were heating up, I poured some almond milk into a glass and got a plate out of the cabinet for the pancakes when they were done.

After I ate breakfast, I decided to do a little bit of yoga to relax. I put on some soft classical music, sat on the living room rug, and took a few deep breaths. I did twenty minutes of intense stretches and poses before I decided to stop. It really did center me and relax my nerves.

I went into my bedroom, picked out my outfit for practice. After I showered and dressed, I sat on my bed. I looked at the pictures around the room of my family throughout the years. I also glanced at the plant my mom gave me when I moved into this apartment. Both of my parents just assumed I would be with a man, and for a while, that was true. But now I didn't know how I felt about that. I didn't know how I was going to tell them I liked a woman or how they would respond to me telling them.

I zoned out a little as I stared at the pictures around the room. I shook my head to snap myself out of my zombie-like state. Even though Sierra was at work and probably doing someone's tattoo, I wanted to let her know my plans to tell Mei that I liked her cousin and wanted her number. Not that I didn't have a reason to lie about it. But when Sierra and I had first discussed this a couple of weeks ago, I'd told her that I would muster up the courage to speak with Mei. So I wanted to let her know today was the day.

Me: Sierra, are you busy?

Sierra: On my break. What's up?

Me: I'm going to do it. I'm going to ask about Lyric.

Sierra: Really? You're finally going to do it?

Me: Yes, even though I'm nervous as hell.

Sierra: Don't be. You got this!

Me: Thanks, Sierra.

Sierra: No problem. I have to get back to work. Keep me posted, okay?

Me: I will.

I put down my phone and took another deep breath. Sierra was the best roommate that I could ever ask for. She didn't judge me when I told her I liked girls. She was nothing but supportive.

I gathered up my dance bag and left for the studio. I arrived around twelve thirty and was greeted by Ms. Brandi with her famous smile shining brightly.

"Hey, Lyric. How's it going this afternoon? You seem a little stressed," she said. She could always read me perfectly.

"I'm okay. Just a lot on my mind," I said.

"Do you want to talk about it?"

"No. It's alright, but thanks, I appreciate it."

Ms. Brandi looked at me for a moment longer, but she didn't probe me any further. I was relieved. I didn't want to get onto the topic of liking girls. Even though she probably heard it all from being our dance "counselor," I wasn't ready to talk about it yet.

I quickly left Ms. Brandi at her desk and walked into the rehearsal room. I put my bag down against the nearest wall and took out my ballet shoes. After I slipped them on, I walked to the barre and started warming up.

After a while, the other dancers started to file into class. I left the barre and sat on the floor, watching the other dancers get situated. Soon, Mei came in and plopped herself down next to me. I acted as if I was watching the remaining dancers come into class.

"Hey, Lyric, you look distracted," Mei said, tapping my shoulder.

"Nah, I'm fine. Just thinking about what Sloane will teach us today."

"Oh? Are you sure that's all? It seems like it might be more than that."

What's with all the damn probing. I mean . . . shit, if I wasn't ready to talk to Mei about Xenia, she would have definitely forced it out of me.

"Well, since you brought it up, I'd like to ask you about Xenia." I swallowed slowly.

"What about her?" Mei cocked her head to the side.

"Umm . . . I may have a little crush on her and want to know if she feels the same," I softly blurted out.

Mei looked at me and gave a half smile. She looked at her ballet slippers and started playing with the ribbon. She seemed like she had something to say but was hesitant to tell me. "Lyric, Xenia and I were talking . . ." Mei trailed off.

"Talking? About what?"

Mei looked at me. "She likes you too, Lyric."

I could have jumped up and ran all around the dance studio. But all I did was smile at this new revelation. "So Xenia wouldn't mind if I asked you for her cell number?" I asked eagerly.

"Umm . . ." Mei hesitated before pulling her cell phone out of her bag.

I pulled out my cell phone and typed in Xenia's number as Mei read it off to me.

"Now, I have to warn you, Lyric. It won't last," she cautioned.

I looked at her in disbelief. Why did she even give me Xenia's number if she felt that way? *What the fuck? Some cousin you are.* But I just bit my tongue, even though I was upset Mei thought that about Xenia's and my possible relationship.

As soon as I finished putting my phone away, Sloane walked in. She looked like she meant business with today's practice. I hoped I could keep up because my mind was focused on finally calling Xenia after class.

I was right. Sloane worked our asses off. I hadn't sweated this profusely during class in a while. It was good though. I needed to get my anxious energy out somehow and what better way than to dance it out.

After class finished, I quickly gathered my things. I was ready to bolt out of there when Mei stopped me.

"Just be careful," Mei said.

"Why? What do you have against Xenia and me dating?" I asked.

"It's not what I have against it. It's just complicated," she said.

I didn't know why Mei was being so vague about this. *What's the problem?* I wondered. Maybe there was no problem. Maybe Mei just wanted to make it seem like there was. Regardless, I was still going to call Xenia.

"Okay, Mei. I gotta go." I left Mei standing there without asking her why it was complicated. I just wanted to make the initial call and take it from there. If Xenia and I were truly meant to be, I didn't care how complicated it would be. We could overcome anything thrown at us. I was certainly up for the challenge. I wasn't going to let what Mei said discourage me from going after who I wanted.

I RUSHED HOME, took a shower, and threw on some comfortable clothes. I grabbed something quick to eat for a late lunch, then contemplated when I would make the call. *The sooner the better*, I thought. But I was so nervous, I started to overthink everything. Even though Mei clearly told me that Xenia liked me and gave me her number, I couldn't help but feel terrified. Xenia was the first girl I'd ever had feelings for. Before that, it was only guys on my radar. *It's now or never.* I picked up my phone, found Xenia's name in my contacts, and pushed the call button.

"Hello?" a voice answered on the other end.

I took a deep breath. "Hello, Xenia?"

"Hi, who's this?"

"It's Lyric. Mei gave me your number. I hope it's alright that I called. Are you busy?

"Oh . . . Hi, Lyric. No, I'm not busy. It's fine that Mei gave you my number. I'm glad, actually."

I could sense Xenia smiling as she spoke that last sentence. It eased my nervousness, and a peace came over my entire body.

"So, what's up?" Xenia asked.

"Well, the reason I'm calling is because I have a little crush on you." I felt my cheeks blushing.

"You do?" There was a hint of excitement in her voice.

"I do. It's really weird for me to admit that actually. I've only liked and dated guys up until this point."

"Same here! You are the first girl I ever had a crush on."

"So where do we go from here?"

"Would you be up to going on a date to see if this might go any further?" Xenia asked.

"Of course I would," I said in the calmest voice ever. On the inside, I had a million butterflies swarming through my stomach. This was the moment I'd been dreaming about since I'd met Xenia.

"Okay, well I'm free this weekend. How about Saturday?"

"This Saturday is perfect," I said. I started to think about day-date ideas. *What could we do? Where could we go?* Then my mind automatically switched into panic mode. *But how do I act? Will it be different than going on a date with a guy?*

What will we talk about? Wait, this is Xenia's first date with a girl too. She's probably just as nervous as me, I thought, trying to calm myself down enough to finish the call on a good beat.

"So, Saturday it is. I have to get going now," Xenia said, breaking me out of my thoughts. "But I'm so happy you called, and I will see you this weekend."

"I'm really looking forward to it, Xenia. Have a great rest of your afternoon. I will see you on Saturday," I said, smiling.

After I got off the call with Xenia, I wanted to tell Sierra how well the conversation went and that we had a date. As soon the thought entered my mind, I heard keys rustling in the door. I made my way out into the living room. Sierra was already locking the door behind her.

"Hey, Sierra. How was work?" I asked.

She turned around. "It was busy. But overall, I had a great day. How was your day?"

"It was fantastic." I couldn't hold back the smile forming on my lips.

"Oh . . . really? Tell me more," Sierra said as we walked into the living room and sat on the couch.

"I have a date on Saturday!" I blurted out.

"I take it this date is not with Zane," she teased.

"Nope. It's with Xenia."

"That's what I figured." Sierra smiled. "Are you nervous?"

"Like hell," I said. "I've never done this before. What if I say the wrong thing? What if she ends up not liking me?" I grabbed a pillow off of the couch and hugged it.

"You are overthinking. It will be totally fine. She will like you. Doesn't she already?" Sierra said.

"Yeah, she does. At least that's what Mei told me," I responded.

"Well then, you have nothing to worry about. Just be yourself."

I let Sierra's last statement sink deep into my brain. I truly didn't have anything to worry about. Mei told me Xenia liked me. Xenia gave off the same vibes when we were talking on the phone. So, I needed to calm my ass down. It was going to be alright.

"Hey listen, I'm going to call it a night," Sierra said. "I'm kind of tired, but I'm so happy for you."

"I should turn in too. It's been a whirlwind of a day. And thank you." I put the pillow back in its proper place on the couch.

"You're welcome. You know I have your back," Sierra said before heading to her bedroom.

"I know."

I ended up watching a little TV in the living room before I went to bed. This day couldn't have gone more perfectly. I couldn't wait to see what Saturday would bring.

THE REST of the week flew by. The anticipation built as the weekend drew closer. Xenia and I spoke on the phone halfway through the week to finalize our date plans. We decided to have lunch at Café Ciel.

I woke up Saturday morning feeling excited, confident, and ready for our date. I decided to wear my black-and-green checkered baggy pants that had large white stripes on them. For my top, I wore a plain white T-shirt and tied a knot in the front. I left my hair down and threw on black wedges. I checked myself over in the mirror. I put on light reddish-brown eye shadow and went with a shiny neutral gloss on my lips.

"Hey, Sierra, what do you think of my outfit?" I asked, standing at her bedroom door as she got ready for work.

She was gathering up some notebooks laying on her bed that were labeled RECENT TATTOO DRAWINGS and putting them in a pocket folder. When she looked toward me, she gasped. "You look so gorgeous!" she exclaimed.

"You think so?"

Sierra smirked. "Oh, yes. Xenia won't know what hit her."

"Thank you. I'm so nervous though." I fiddled with the knot on my shirt.

"Why? You have so much to offer and have no reason to be nervous. Don't sell yourself short. Xenia wouldn't have agreed to go on a date if she didn't think you two would hit it off."

"That's true. I'm just worried I won't make a good impression."

Sierra walked over and swatted me with her notebook. "Lyric, please. Please get out of your head. You'll impress her. You have nothing to worry about."

"Hey . . . ouch," I rubbed my shoulder where the notebook hit me. "Okay. I promise I won't self-sabotage myself or this date with negative thoughts."

"Now that's what I'm talking about. Be confident."

"Thank you, Sierra. I'm going to finish getting ready."

"You're welcome. I have to finish getting my things ready too. You're going to be fine."

I left Sierra's bedroom and went back into my room. When I was about to leave, I shot Xenia a quick text to tell her I was on my way to the café. We both decided that we would drive in our own cars just in case the date didn't go well and one of us wanted to bail. I doubted that would be the case, but we wanted to give each other that option.

WHEN I ARRIVED at Café Ciel, I chose a table closest to the window. I sat down, grabbed my phone, and started scrolling through social media. It helped calm my anxiety for some odd reason. The server stopped by the table, and I let her know I had gotten here early and was waiting for my date. The second time she stopped by, I ordered two glasses of water. I checked the time—12:50 p.m. Xenia and I had agreed on one. *She still has ten more minutes. Why am I being so paranoid that she won't show?*

As soon as I returned to scrolling through my phone, the chimes on the café door rang. I looked up to see Xenia walking toward me. My breath caught in my throat. Her jet-black hair was straight and hung past her shoulders. She wore a light-wash jean jacket over a white top that showed off her midriff ever so slightly. Her jeans were also a light wash with various color patches sewn on. Black open-toed wedges completed the outfit.

"I thought I was going to get here before you." Xenia sat across from me.

"Oh, I try to be on time or early. But I see we are both on the same page when it comes to being early for things."

The server brought our waters to the table while I tried not to focus on how hard Xenia's nipples were poking out beneath her tank.

"Oh . . . thanks for ordering the waters ahead of time." She took a sip.

"Would you like to order now?" the server asked.

"Sure."

We each gave her our order and as soon as she left, Xenia and I stared bashfully at each other. *What is she thinking?*

Finally, I broke the staring and silence. "So . . . umm . . . how is the orchestra going?"

"It's going well. We've been practicing some new pieces in preparation for our next performance, whenever that is." Her eyes sparkled with curiosity. "How's dance going?"

"That's great. I can't wait to see you perform again." I smiled, which made her blush. "Dance is going well. Sloane, our dance instructor, has been working us hard."

Xenia chuckled, the sound evaporating more of the nervousness. "I definitely know how that is. Mr. Charles is a perfectionist, especially since we practice most of the pieces he wrote. He just wants us as an orchestra to perform the pieces right."

The date was going well. I felt an even stronger connection as we talked more about the creative aspect of our professions. It seemed like, artistically, both of us shared similar ways of thinking and viewing the world around us. But what I was really curious about was our families and how they would react to us dating. I wanted to know whether her family would have a problem with me being a woman, and a Black woman at that. Talking to Mei about the situation didn't ease my worries, it only amplified them. I wanted to hear Xenia's thoughts. If they didn't accept me, would she still want to continue seeing me? Would she be bold enough to see past their ignorance to not let it affect our relationship in any way?

"Xenia, can I ask you a question?" I asked during a natural lull in the conversation.

"Sure, anything," she said.

"I was wondering . . . how will your family react if we start dating?"

Xenia took a sip of her water and sighed. "Umm . . ." It looked like she wanted to say something, but she was silent.

Xenia looked down at her glass of water and began playing with the straw.

So I chimed in, "I don't know how my family would react. Since they both work in the entertainment industry, I hope they would be accepting, but it's hard to tell."

"Oh . . ." She didn't say anything else.

I looked at Xenia, and she looked back at me with an unreadable expression on her face. I heard her shoes tapping on the floor a few times. She grabbed a piece of her hair and started to twirl it around her finger. Even though I wanted to know what her family would think of us dating, I didn't want to push her into talking about it if she didn't want to. We were still in the beginning stages of getting to know one another, so I could understand her apprehension about telling me certain things.

Our food arrived, and we both dug in. I guessed we could blame it on first date jitters. We practically inhaled our food. After we finished, we glanced at our empty plates and laughed.

Xenia's eyes went wide. "Oh my. I guess I was really that hungry."

"I guess I was too," I echoed.

We called the server over to bring the bill for our food. We opted to pay separately since it was our first date. After we paid, we stood and I gave Xenia a hug. She fell right into me and wrapped her arms tightly around my waist. Being in her arms felt like home. I could have stayed there forever.

Eventually, we broke apart and smiled shyly at one another.

"I had a great time," I said. "I would love to go out with you again, if that's something you would like?"

Xenia was quiet for a few seconds before responding. "I

had a great time too. I would love to go on another date with you, most definitely." She smiled brightly.

"What would you like to do for the second date?"

"Maybe we could go to a paint-and-sip class or to a pottery-making class," Xenia suggested.

"That's sounds like fun," I said. "But one more thing. If we end up becoming official, I want Café Ciel to be our spot. The place we come back to on each anniversary we have."

"Deal. Café Ciel will officially be our spot." Xenia hugged me again.

CHAPTER 8

Xenia

T ime flew when you were with the person you were supposed to be with. I never in a million years would have fathomed Lyric and I would be celebrating our two-month anniversary. After we went back to Café Ciel to celebrate two months as a couple, I invited Lyric over to my apartment. I didn't know what would actually happen when we got to my apartment, but I was down for anything Lyric was willing to do. I really liked her and couldn't wait to show her how much I did. I was hoping maybe tonight would be the night. After we came through the front door of my apartment, we removed our shoes.

Lyric looked around. "Your apartment is so warm and cozy."

"Thank you," I said.

"Can I see your bedroom?" Lyric asked. She looked at me coyly.

"Right now? Don't you want to watch a movie or something?" I was surprised by her boldness. I didn't know she had this "I'm in charge" nature about her, but I kind of liked it.

Lyric bit her bottom lip and shook her head. She clearly

had one thing on her mind. I wasn't mad at that; I wanted it too. I led Lyric to my bedroom.

She glanced around and motioned me to my bed. "Lie down," she said firmly.

I did exactly what she instructed. When I was on the bed, Lyric climbed on and straddled me, pressing herself against me. She started grinding slowly, then picked up speed. The friction between us was electric. I could feel myself already getting wet. She continued this for an exhilarating few minutes and then stopped.

"What?" I asked as I lay there, wet between my thighs.

Lyric leaned down and put her lips on mine, kissing me long and hard, trailing her hands to the waistband of my jeans. She urgently fumbled with the button, trying to undo it. I quickly moved her hands away and undid the button for her. She ran her fingers through my hair.

Breaking our kiss, Lyric lifted her shirt over her head, exposing a sheer, pink lace bra. Her breasts were perky and her nipples already hard. I reached to touch them, but she firmly shook her head, ordering me to wait. I so wanted to touch her breasts, but I kind of liked Lyric bossing me around, and I obeyed. Lyric stood up and removed her jeans. She motioned for me to get off the bed. I stood. Lyric lifted my shirt over my head and threw it on the floor. She unclasped my bra with only a little trouble. Next, she started pulling down my unbuttoned jeans. I shimmied out of them while she pulled. Once they were off, Lyric knelt in front of me. She looked up at me with a mischievous grin and a sparkle in her eyes. Heat spread throughout my entire body as she used her teeth to pull down my panties. When they were on the ground, I stepped out of them, now completely naked. Lyric rose to meet me and gently pushed me back on the bed. With her panties still on, she crawled on top of me, spread my legs, and started rubbing herself against my bare pussy.

"Oh God," I moaned.

It was ecstasy. That was the only way to describe the pure bliss I felt while she was fucking me with her panties on.

"Take them off," I managed to say between moans.

Lyric rolled away and slid her panties off. In only her bra, she climbed back on top of me, pressing all her weight into me, and continued to grind against me with her newly bare pussy. *Holy shit. This feels like heaven.* We intertwined like a symphony as the rhythmic sound of our panting and moaning filled the air.

"Xenia. Shit, baby, you feel like a dream," Lyric whispered in my ear. She continued to fuck me harder and faster.

"I'm going to come!" I was practically screaming.

"Wait, don't. Not yet!"

I gave her a desperate look. "I'm going to fucking come."

Lyric slid down my body and between my legs. She started to play with my clit, massaging it with her fingers. I closed my eyes. After a while longer, I felt something wet between my folds. Lyric was fucking me with her tongue, moving it in and out and in circular motions.

I couldn't take it anymore. I was going to come.

"Go ahead. Come, baby." Lyric gave the command.

Without hesitation, I came. Lyric kept licking and sucking on me. Savoring what I just released on her tongue.

Next, Lyric moved back up my body and gently kneaded my breasts. Little moans escaped my mouth. She proceeded to kiss me again, allowing me to taste my sweetness on her lips.

"I'm not done with you yet, babe," Lyric said, and she put two fingers inside me.

"Holy shit," I cried out as she moved her fingers inside me.

"You like that?"

"Yes!" I arched my back. The pleasure was so fucking amazing.

Lyric continued finger-fucking me, and I slowly became putty in her hands. After I came a second time, she collapsed by my side. Breathing heavily, she smirked.

"Babe, do you know how good you made me feel?" I asked.

"No, but I heard. And that was enough for me."

Lyric played with my hair, twirling it around her fingers. I lay there, a sense of dread encroaching on my bliss. The last two months had been amazing, but I knew the end was likely coming. But I didn't want to give this up. *It's not fair. I don't want what Lyric and I have to end. It's not a phase. This is so real, realer than any of my past relationships with guys. I'm scared. I don't want to forget Lyric or this moment. I can't take back what I feel for her. I wouldn't want to. She is it for me, but what shitty timing this is.*

Lyric looked in my eyes and saw my hesitation. "What's wrong?"

"Lyric, there's something I need to tell you. I haven't been totally honest with you."

"What do you mean?"

I was terrified. I didn't know how she'd take what I was about to tell her. I didn't want to break her heart. That was the last thing I wanted to do. I looked in her eyes to see if she was trying to anticipate what I was going to say, even though there was no way she would have a clue about what I was going to say. I swallowed so hard that a lump formed in my throat. I was trying to hold back tears.

"I will be getting engaged soon," I said. I felt my heart breaking in a million pieces.

Lyric sat up. "What? Engaged? To who?"

"His name is Jun Lee. My parents chose him for me. It's an arranged marriage."

Lyric let out a laugh and shook her head in disbelief. "Seriously? Your parents chose him for you to marry. Are you fucking kidding me? Wait, so, what the hell is this? What are we? What was this?" She motioned between us.

I sat on my knees. "This was the best night of my life. You are very special to me, don't you know that? I wouldn't have thought twice about being in your arms, being here with you. I'm so sorry, but I don't have a choice."

"Do you know how stupid you sound right now?" Lyric's expression went cold as she raised her voice. "You don't have a choice? You do! You don't have to marry him."

"I'm afraid I do." I looked down so I didn't have to see the emotions bared on her face. I leaned back against the headboard and wrapped my arms around my knees.

"I think I'm going to go." Lyric got off my bed and started to dress.

I watched her as tears ran down my face. I knew I had to tell her the truth, but I wish I could have kept this a secret forever. I felt panic at the thought of losing her.

"Please don't go," I pleaded.

Ignoring me, Lyric finished getting dressed. She turned and looked at me, tears in her eyes.

Shit.

"Have a nice fucking life with Jun Lee." Lyric stormed out of my room, slamming the door shut behind her.

All I could do was lie there. Lyric was beyond pissed, and I couldn't blame her. With tear-filled eyes, I curled into a fetal position, rocking myself back and forth. I felt hollow inside. Like a large stone took the place of my heart. I didn't want to feel bitter because I had no right to be. But I did. I wanted Lyric to hear me out and know that my entire being was wrapped up in her. I let out a scream, hoping my neighbors wouldn't hear. Though at this point, I didn't really care if they heard. I needed to release all the tension I was feeling. I felt helpless that I had no choice in the matter when it came to marrying Jun Lee. Maybe I shouldn't have started dating Lyric knowing that. But a part of me wanted to escape that reality, hoping that Lyric and I somehow could have had a future together.

This was the mind game I'd been playing. I'd convinced myself that by being with Lyric, I wouldn't have to marry him. In reality though, no matter who I dated, I would marry him. Especially if the person I wanted to be with was of the same gender. Like Mei said, there was no way my mom would go for that. It would be easier to convince them if Lyric was a guy. A similar scenario to Mei and Qiang's love story. But I didn't want a love story like my cousin. And I certainly didn't want a love story that was put together by my parents either. But what choice did I have? None.

I sat up and wiped the tears from my eyes with the back of my hand. I had to talk to someone about what just happened. I thought about inviting Mei over, but that quickly left a sour taste in my mouth. *Who can I call?* Then it dawned on me— Brielle. She had been pretty supportive when I'd first told her about Lyric. I grabbed my cell off the nightstand and texted Brielle.

Me: *Hey, Bri. Are you busy? I need someone to talk to. Can you come over?*

I got up and dressed while I waited for Brielle to text me back. I put on different clothes, so I didn't have to think about what had just happened between Lyric and me. I also decided to wash my comforter set. I didn't want Lyric's scent on my sheets. I ripped the comforter and sheets from my bed, promptly walked to the laundry room, threw them into the washing machine, and turned it on. As soon as I left the laundry room, my phone vibrated.

Brielle: *No, not busy. I'll be right over. I hope everything's okay.*

I didn't reply to her message. I just continued to straighten up my apartment. After I was satisfied with the results, I sat on the couch and blankly stared into the void. I fucked up badly. I didn't know why I wasn't honest with Lyric from the beginning. That was a lie. I knew why; I was selfish. I didn't want to lose her and what we had. Lyric wouldn't have wanted to date me even if she'd known I was about to get engaged. So, either way, I would have lost her, sooner or later.

A knock at the door jolted me out of my thoughts. "Shit," I mumbled as I got up, startled from the noise.

"Hey, Bri, thanks for coming," I said when I opened the door.

"No problem. You look like shit." Brielle looked me up and down.

"Geez . . . thanks for the encouragement," I said sarcastically. "Come on in. Do you want some wine?"

She came in and plopped down on my couch. "Sure."

I poured two glasses of wine and walked back into the living room. I handed her a glass and sat beside her.

"Thanks. So what's on your mind?" Bri asked.

I sighed and took a sip of wine. Brielle looked at me as I was trying to gather my thoughts. She didn't rush me to tell her what I was troubled about. She just waited patiently.

"Lyric and I celebrated our two-month anniversary today," I said. "We went back to Café Ciel and had a great time. I invited her back here, and we had sex for the first time."

"Oh . . . okay. That sounds like it went well, right?" Brielle looked puzzled.

"Yeah, if you leave out the part after when I told her I was getting engaged soon."

"Wait, what? Engaged?"

"Yes. I'm getting engaged to a man I've never even met." I could feel tears welling up.

She took another sip of her wine and went quiet for a few seconds. "So . . . how did Lyric take the news that you were getting engaged?"

"Not good. She stormed out of here so fucking fast."

"I'm sorry. I know you like her so much."

"I really fucked up, Brielle."

"Maybe you didn't. Do you have to marry this man?"

"I'm afraid I do. There's no way around it." I grabbed the pillow off my couch and hugged it while I stared blankly ahead.

"You can't talk it over with your parents?"

"If I could, I would have done that by now. They'll disown me, Bri, since Lyric isn't a guy," I explained.

"Let me see if I understand. They would rather have you be miserably married to a man that you even don't know but are expecting you to love, than be happy in a relationship that is a little unconventional?" She drained her glass of wine.

I nodded.

"That's not love. Your parents should love you enough to want you to be with whoever makes you happy. It shouldn't matter what gender they are," she said.

"I know."

I didn't want to start crying again, especially not in front of Brielle. But like a dam, the tears unleashed a nonstop flow. Brielle reached over and embraced me. I cried harder as all the emotions from everything that was happening rose to the surface.

"Shit. I'm sorry . . . I didn't—" I started to say before Bri cut me off.

"Shh . . . you're allowed to feel, Xenia. There's nothing wrong with crying."

"But I didn't want it to come to this. I don't want to lose her," I muttered through my tears.

"I know you don't. But unless you find a way to explain the situation to your parents, what else can you do?

I sighed. Mei was right all along. I had to take the easier way out. Even though the "easier" way was awful. It would cost me the woman I loved, and I would have to embark on an unknown future with a man I didn't even know.

Brielle picked up the remote and turned on the TV. She started flipping through the channels, landing on Comedy Central.

"You need a good laugh," Brielle said.

I did need a good laugh. Laughter was healing for the soul. I definitely needed some soul healing. When I glanced at the TV, it was Margaret Cho, one of my favorite comedians. She was performing one of her recent stand-ups and, as usual, was hilarious.

"Thanks for turning this shitty night into something better, Brielle," I told her during the commercial break.

"That's what I'm here for. To help you through the worst of the worst of days," she said.

"I'm so grateful for your friendship and how you want to be there for me."

"I'm grateful to be your friend and to be able to be here for you too. I want nothing but the best for you." She hugged me.

CHAPTER 9

Lyric

How can I be such a fucking idiot? This was not how I was expecting my and Xenia's two-month anniversary date to go. I kept wondering about the clues I'd missed as I was driving back to my apartment. *Is that the reason Mei was being so vague about Xenia the day I asked for her number?* She didn't want to tell me that Xenia was going to be getting engaged. *Oh . . . fuck . . . that is exactly why.* I clearly remembered Mei telling me that our relationship wouldn't last. *Shit . . . instead of asking her why, I just ignored that obvious red flag.* It was right there, plain as day. I had no one to blame but myself. Xenia had plenty of time to be honest about her upcoming engagement, but she chose not to. Even though I was the one that fucked her tonight, she literally fucked me over with her dishonesty.

When I got to my apartment, I opened my front door as quietly as possible. I didn't want to wake up Sierra. She would want to hear how the date went, and that was the last thing I wanted to talk about right now. But I also knew keeping it bottled up wasn't going to help me either. Maybe Sierra could give me some sound advice on what I should do.

I put my car keys on the kitchen table, grabbed a glass of water, chugged it down, and went to my room. I changed into my pajamas and climbed into bed. *Fuck this day to hell.* As soon as my head hit my pillow, the tears started to flow. My heart felt like it was being weighed down by a ton of bricks. Eventually, I cried myself to sleep.

THE NEXT MORNING, I woke up feeling like shit. I got out of bed and put on my robe and slippers. I looked at myself in the full-length mirror I have on my door. That was a mistake. Not only did I feel like shit, I looked like it too. I forgot to put my satin bonnet on before I went to bed last night and now my hair was all over the place. My eyes were puffy, plus I had dark circles under my eyes. There were streaks of tearstains on my face. This was the worst I had ever looked after a breakup. I usually had no problem moving on from most of the guys I'd dated in the past. But there was something different about Xenia. Even though I had no choice, I didn't want to let go of her.

I ventured into the kitchen to get a bowl of cereal for breakfast. I sat at the table to eat my cereal and couldn't keep my mind off what happened between Xenia and me. I desperately needed to get my thoughts down on paper. I was feeling hurt, betrayed, lied to, and flat out disregarded. While I was still ruminating through my thoughts, Sierra came into the kitchen.

"Morning," she said.

"Morning," I said in a monotone voice without looking at her.

Sierra started making her morning coffee and grabbed two

protein bars out of the pantry cabinet. After her coffee was ready, she joined me at the table. "What's wrong?"

"Nothing. Why do you think something's wrong with me?"

"Well, for starters, the way you just said 'good morning' while staring off into space."

"Aren't you quite the detective this morning?" I said sarcastically.

"Lyric, seriously. What's up?" Her voice was steady and unwavering.

I put my spoon down and sighed. I didn't know how I would begin to tell her what happened last night without crying. But there was no point in lying. She'd already noticed I wasn't my normal self.

"Xenia and I broke up," I finally said.

"What? What happened? Wasn't it your anniversary yesterday?" she asked.

"Yes. We went back to the café and had a great time . . ." I drifted off at the memory.

"Then?"

"Xenia invited me back to her apartment, and we had sex. It was amazing. But afterward, she proceeded to tell me that she's getting engaged." I shook my head in disbelief, still not wanting to accept this fact.

"Engaged? What the hell?! So she was playing you all along." Sierra's eyes went wide.

"Apparently."

"So, what did you do after she told you?" She got up from the table and got some orange juice.

"I immediately left," I said.

"Good. She lied. Xenia doesn't deserve you." She sat back down at the table, taking a sip of her juice.

"I know. It's just hard. I really liked her . . . maybe even started to love her," I confessed. "Now what am I going to do?"

"Oh, Lyric, I'm so sorry. But there are a lot of people in this world. A lot of genuine, sincere people that would love to date you. Don't give up," Sierra said.

"Like Zane," I said knowing that's who she meant by "a lot of people."

"I didn't specifically mean him. But since you brought him up . . ."

"Sierra, I know you. You sure as hell meant Zane." I raised an eyebrow . "I was thinking . . . but it might be too late."

"Too late for what? To take him up on his offer for a date?"

"Yes," I said, matter-of-factly.

"Well, you'll never know until you ask him. Maybe dating him will take your mind of Xenia. You need to focus your attention and time on someone else. But there's also a possibility that it may backfire and make you miss her more," she said honestly.

"I know. You're right. I guess I'll have to take my chances."

"So are you going to call him?" she asked.

"I might. I'm not totally sure yet."

"Take your time. There's no rush."

I thought about the situation. Sierra was right. I definitely needed to take my mind off Xenia. Zane was the perfect guy to do that. I did have a great time with Sierra and him at the concert a few months back and at the diner. I was processing things that night, so it wouldn't have been fair to go out with him then. Even now, I didn't know how fair it would be since it was basically a rebound date. *Fuck it. I only live once, right?*

"I think I'll call Zane right now," I said.

"Are you sure?" Sierra asked. "What if he's dating someone?

"I appreciate your concern. But if he is dating someone else, then I'll move on to plan B."

"What's your plan B?"

"I really don't have one," I told her honestly.

"Well, we are going to hope for the best. You got this."

"Thanks, I'll let you know how it goes." I got up from the table and went to my bedroom for some privacy.

I stood in my room, going over what I would say. *What if he's like, "Why are you calling now?" Or what if he is dating someone else? Get out of your head and just go for it, Lyric.* I still had Zane's number from when Sierra gave it to me after we'd left the diner that night, just in case I changed my mind. I found his number in my phone and pushed the call button. It rang a few times before Zane picked up.

"Hello?" he answered.

"Hey, Zane, it's Lyric. How have you been doing?"

"Hey, Lyric. I'm doing good. I don't normally answer numbers I don't know," he stated.

Strike one. Sierra didn't even mention to Zane that she gave me his number. Maybe he would have expected my call. Damn you, Sierra. Why am I acting so desperate? What the fuck is wrong with me?

"Oh . . . I'm sorry. I didn't mean to—" I started to say before he cut me off.

"No . . . no. You're good. It's no big deal. I'm just relaxing. So, what's up?" he asked.

"I was calling to see if your offer to go on a date with me still stands. I was going through some things before. But I'm fine now."

"Oh, the date. Yes, I would love to take you out," he said excitedly. "When are you free?"

"Is this afternoon too soon?" I asked hesitantly.

"This afternoon? That's perfect. I know this new indoor rock-climbing place called Off the Cliff that I've always wanted to try."

"Oh . . . that sounds like fun. I've never gone rock climbing before."

"Great. Text me your address, and I'll pick you up around noon," he said.

"Okay. Let me get dressed, then I'll text you my address."

After we hung up, I looked through my closet for something to wear to go rock climbing. I was searching through my assortment of tops and jeans when I heard Sierra's footsteps.

"Hey, I was waiting for you to come back out to tell me what happened with the call," Sierra said. She seemed a little annoyed.

"Oh . . . I'm sorry. We are going to an indoor rock-climbing place at noon."

"That's awesome. I'm happy for you. This is a good thing." She sounded more cheerful.

"Are you sure?"

"Yes. You need to get your mind off her. You'll have a great time with Zane. You already know you have dance in common." She shifted her weight from one foot to the other as she stood at my door.

"Yeah, that *is* a plus."

"Trust me, you'll wish you would have chosen him over Xenia."

"I don't know about that."

"All I'm saying is don't overthink it. Let things happen naturally."

Let things happen naturally. Sierra always had the right words to say to calm my anxious mind. I would go on this date and have a great time. *I won't expect anything to happen that I won't want to. I'm in control.*

After Sierra left my room, I resumed my search to find an outfit for the date. I settled on black leggings, a purple sports bra underneath a loose sleeveless black T-shirt, and my purple-and-black sneakers. After I dressed, I put my hair in a high ponytail and put on some neutral lip gloss. When I was finished, I texted Zane my address.

While waiting for Zane to arrive, I checked my social media and scrolled past Xenia's Instagram. I couldn't help but wonder if she was thinking of me. Last night had to be as special to her as it was to me. It was the first time either of us had had sex with a woman. We were each other's first. That's another reason why I was so hurt and pissed at her. *How, after all that happened, could you want to marry that man, whoever he is?* But I guessed I didn't mean as much to her as I thought I did.

While I was on my phone, Zane texted that he was outside my apartment. I hurried to grab my sling bag and threw it over my shoulder. I was all set. I poked my head in Sierra's room. "I'm leaving now."

"Have fun. And remember, no overthinking," she said, pointing at me.

"Thanks, no overthinking."

I stepped out of my apartment. The weather was perfect. It was in the low seventies, and a gentle breeze was blowing. I took a deep breath in and out. *I can do this.*

I opened Zane's passenger door and got in. "Hey," I said.

"Hey. You ready?" he said.

I buckled my seatbelt. "Yup. Thanks for getting me out of my apartment. It was a rough twenty-four hours."

"Oh . . . really? Roommate problems?" Zane pulled off down the street.

"Umm . . . not quite." *Why had I mentioned it?*

"Well, hopefully rock climbing will take your mind off things." He smiled.

"Hopefully." I smiled back.

When we arrived, we pulled in a parking space. When Zane stepped out of his car, I got a better look at what he was wearing. He had on navy track pants with two white strips running down each side of his pant legs. He had on a loose white T-shirt and navy running shoes. Zane's blond hair was spiked up with gel. He did look handsome. But I couldn't trust my feelings. I didn't know if I wanted to think he looked handsome because I was trying to take my mind off Xenia or if that was what I truly thought.

When Zane and I entered the building, I was taken back by how high the rock-climbing walls were. I looked at Zane wide-eyed. "I don't think I can do this."

He chuckled lightly. "You'll be fine. It's not that hard to rock climb. Don't let the high walls discourage you into believing you can't because you certainly can."

People of all ages were climbing on the walls in harnesses. Zane and I watched them for a few minutes before we got in the line to pay for our own rock-climbing session.

It was thirty dollars each for a thirty-minute time slot. Zane paid for both of us. I said I could pay for myself, but he insisted. I wasn't going to argue with that. After he paid, we got harnessed up and started looking for a wall.

"How about here?" Zane said as we walked around the building, trying to find a near-empty wall.

"Here is fine." I looked up at the wall we were about to climb.

I went to one side of the wall, and Zane went to the other side.

"Let's race," he said.

"Umm . . . okay . . . I don't know how fast I can go since I've never done this before."

"Are you up for it or not?" There was a twinkle in his eye.

I smirked. "Let's go then."

We both got into position. Then we heard a whistle. Even though I was sure it wasn't for us, we both started to climb. I struggled to grip the first few spaces designated for my feet. But I eventually got the hang of it and began making my way up the wall. I didn't really care all that much about racing. I was content on moving at the pace that I was comfortable with. As soon as I reached the top of the wall, I heard Zane's voice. He was already going back down.

"Congrats. You made it," he yelled.

I let go of the top and made my way down the wall. When I reached where Zane was standing, I was out of breath. "Thanks."

"Come on. Let's get some water," he said.

We stopped by a concession booth and paid for two bottles of water and sat at a table.

"So, what did you think?" he asked as he opened his water bottle.

"This was fun. I'm glad you suggested we come here."

"I'm glad you finally decided to come on a date with me." Zane smiled.

I drank some of my water and looked around at the surroundings. This wasn't a bad date. I was enjoying it. But it wasn't the same. I still missed Xenia.

"What are thinking about?" He must have noticed me staring into space.

"Oh, nothing . . . thank you for inviting me even though I turned you down the first time."

"Of course. I wasn't going to hold that against you."

As soon as we finished with our water, we decided to

leave. We got in his car and started heading back to my apartment. When he pulled in front of my driveway, Zane put his car in park.

"I really enjoy hanging out with you this afternoon," he said.

"Me too. It was fun. I had a blast trying something new."

"I was wondering if maybe we could go out again. Next time to dinner?"

"Umm . . . let me think about it." I unbuckled my seatbelt and opened the car door.

"Sure . . . okay," he said, looking kind of confused.

"Bye, Zane. Thanks." I got out of the car, closed the door, and started walking to my front door. I didn't look back, but I heard his car pull away. I was torn. I didn't want to feel like I was leading Zane on, but I also didn't want to hold on to Xenia knowing there was no way we could be together.

CHAPTER 10

Xenia

T oday was going to be a full day of traveling to Shanghai, China, for the beginning of my engagement to Jun Lee. My family and I were going to spend a few days visiting my grandparents and other family members in China. Then I was going to finally meet Jun Lee and his family and have the engagement ceremony. Everything was going to take place over the five days we were going to be China. I didn't know how I felt. *Hollow and numb, I guess.* It had been several weeks since Lyric and I broke up. But I still thought about her often. I also wondered if she thought of me. I wished I could talk to her and explain myself, but it was too late. *Once I'm engaged, Lyric will finally be a distant memory*, I thought. We can put everything we did together in a box on the shelf of my memory. I decided that I would start being intentional and force myself not to think about it.

I sat next to Mei on the plane. My dad was already in Shanghai, so Aunt Tao and Mom sat next to each other across the aisle. For the first few hours, I stared out the window and listened to music on my AirPods. I didn't want to talk to Mei.

because I didn't want to get into how I was really feeling. Plus, she didn't know what went down between Lyric and me. But, as I closed my eyes to drift off to sleep, I felt a tap on my shoulder. I opened my eyes.

"Xen, your engagement ceremony is going to be so beautiful," Mei said.

"How do you know?" I asked.

"Well, Aunt Ai and Mom told me that the ceremony is going to take place at Flower Garden Park. There will be a massive amount of cherry blossom trees."

"Oh, so they told you first and not me, the bride-to-be," I said, annoyed.

"Well after that initial conversation we had that day at the house, we decided that we needed to start planning right away. When you didn't come back for the discussions we had after that, we assumed you wanted us to just plan things for you. If you weren't trying to avoid us, then maybe you would have known," Mei said.

I looked at her and shook my head before turning back to face the window. I hated the fact that Mei knew me so well. Sure, I was avoiding the notion of my impending engagement, but this was also my life. They never should have gone ahead and planned everything without me. Apparently, they didn't care whether I was involved. I was learning more about Mei and the way she handled things. Especially Mei, she should know better, but it was clear now that she didn't really care about how I felt or what I thought. When Mei's parents planned her ceremonies to Qiang, it was different because she knew him, so they could plan together. *I don't know why I'm going willingly into this engagement. It seems like Mei is reveling in the fact that she had more input with my ceremonies than I had with hers.*

"Well I have a life, which I guess you guys don't seem to care about," I said after looking out the window for a few moments.

"If we didn't care about your life as a violinist, we would have never come to see you perform. We definitely support your career."

"But *you* won't support who I want to love and be with."

"Lyric, we've already discussed this. I told you if you don't want to be disowned, take the easy way out. I thought that's what you decided, because here we are, on our way to China."

I just sighed. Mei would never understand. Our stories were totally different. She was allowed to marry the man she'd fallen in love with. Even though the family had disagreed in the beginning, she'd still ended up happily married to Qiang. *I won't get to experience being happy with someone I choose to marry. I will always be miserable. Even if later down the line, I end up falling in love with Jun Lee, I will always think about Lyric and what could have been.*

I didn't talk to Mei for the rest of the flight.

ONCE WE LANDED, we went through customs and then waited in the luggage claim for our suitcases. My mom told us that our cousin Daiyu and her husband, Huan, would be picking us up from the airport. Daiyu was thirty-four, and Huan was thirty-five. They both lived with our grandparents and helped take care of them. They had a boy and a girl, who were three and five years old. I couldn't wait to meet Hu. He hadn't been born yet when Mei had her wedding and Fei had just been a baby. So, it would be exciting to see them and finally get to meet Hu.

"What time will Daiyu and Huan arrive to pick us up?" Mei asked.

"In a few minutes. I told her what time we would be landing," my mom said.

"I can't wait to see Fei and finally meet Hu. Since they are the closest to grandchildren I will have," Aunt Tao said, rolling her eyes.

"Oh, Mom, really?" Mei asked.

"Well, maybe seeing them and how cute they are will change your mind," Aunt Tao said.

"Let's just focus on, Xenia, please. It's her special week." Mei smiled at me.

I gave her a wry smile. I really didn't want to go through with this engagement and soon-to-be wedding. *It is what it is. I wish I had a say it this whole thing.* But even if I did have a say, it wouldn't matter. Not in my case.

After we got our bags, we walked to the airport entrance to wait on our cousins. Mom, Mei, and Aunt Tao were discussing my engagement details. I should have been listening to know what was going on, but I zoned out thinking about Lyric. I wondered what she was doing while I was halfway around the world. She obviously didn't know when I would be getting engaged. I didn't think she would care. But I still adored her and wondered how she was coping with all of this.

Springtime in China was very beautiful. It didn't compare to the photos I saw in the photo albums that my mom and Aunt Tao had of them growing up. Mei and Qiang's wedding had been in the fall. So I knew what fall weather was like in China, but this was my first time here in the spring.

"They're here," Aunt Tao said, pointing to an SUV.

We walked toward the SUV, put our suitcases in the back, and got in.

"Buckle up, everyone," Daiyu told us before Huan pulled off.

All of us did what she said and sat back to enjoy the ride to their house.

"So how was the flight?" Daiyu asked after a while.

"It wasn't too bad. All of us mostly slept," my mom said.

"I forgot how long the flight was," Aunt Tao said.

"Well, it's good that you slept then. It probably made it go faster," Daiyu added. "So are you ready for this week, Xenia? It's a whole large celebration. Your dad has been talking with Jun Lee and his family. Everyone is so excited."

My dad—Matthew, or Manchu as his friends called him—had arrived a week earlier to finalize things with Jun Lee and his family. I had a close relationship with my dad, but it was a different type of closeness than I had with my mom. He had been very affectionate toward me while I was growing up. He always hugged and kissed me and consistently told me that I was loved and beautiful. But he had a hard time expressing the way he felt about certain topics, like boys. He always left those things up to my mom to talk about with me.

But when it had been time for my mom and him to find my future husband, my dad had wanted to make sure that the man I was going to marry could be open and talk. Since he had trouble talking about those things, my dad told me it was important for him to find someone for me that could. Especially when I had children, he wanted our children to have a father that wasn't afraid to be vulnerable. I was so grateful for my dad in that respect. He knew what he lacked as a parent and just wanted the best for me and my future children.

"Ready as I'll ever be," I responded.

Mei glared at me and quickly added, "Oh, she's just nervous. You know how Qiang and I were for our engagement ceremony and wedding."

"You have nothing to be nervous about. I've heard great things about Jun Lee. He's a real gentleman." Daiyu looked back at me and smiled.

I smiled back, knowing in my heart that no matter how wonderful Jun Lee was, he wasn't Lyric. Nobody could ever compare to her. Maybe I was biased because she was the first woman I'd ever been in a relationship with. But instead, I was here in China getting ready for my engagement ceremony.

For the rest of the ride, I glanced out the window at the beautiful flowers on the trees and people walking to their various destinations.

Awhile later, we finally pulled in the driveway of a medium-sized house. It was gray with white shutters and a bright red door. As we were riding through the neighborhood, I had noticed a few houses here and there had red doors. Now I could really see the significance of why my parents had chosen a red door on their house in America. It was not just the fact that a red door represented luck, health, joy, and happiness; it also represented the preservation of a cultural tradition and was a reminder of where they had come from.

"Here we are," Huan said as we sat in the driveway.

"This is a different house than the one we visited five years ago," my mom said.

"I know. We wanted a bigger house when I became pregnant with Hu. It has more room for visitors," Daiyu said.

"Oh, well, it's a nice size. How many rooms does it have?" Aunt Tao asked.

"It has six bedrooms," Daiyu told her.

"Wow!"

"Shall we go in?" Huan unbuckled his seatbelt.

"Let's go," my mom said.

We got our suitcases and walked inside.

"Just put your stuff here for now." Daiyu pointed to a space by the couch. "We'll show you where you'll be sleeping later."

"Are you guys hungry? We made a chicken with broccoli and rice."

"Sure. Thank you," my mom said. "Why don't you show the girls where they'll be sleeping. Tao and I will get everything ready."

"Good idea, Aunt Ai," Daiyu said. Mei and I followed Daiyu down the hall. "Here we are," she said.

We stepped into the room. The walls were white with gold Chinese lettering on them and a king bed with a gold comforter set on it. There was a spacious closet and a white dresser. After Mei and I put our clothes away, we left the room.

"Where's Fei and Hu?" I asked as we walked into the kitchen.

"They're with Huan's parents. I knew there would be a lot of things going on this week so my mother-in-law offered to watch them," Daiyu explained.

"Oh. I wanted to see them," I said.

"They'll be at the engagement ceremony. You'll get a chance to see them then." She smiled.

I knew Mei was glad that Fei and Hu weren't here. Because that meant she wouldn't be hounded by her mom in regard to having children. I wasn't looking forward to that happening to me either.

"Hey, my cherry blossom," my dad said as I came into the living room.

"Hi, Dad. How are you?" I embraced him.

"I'm great. I've been in conversations all week with Jun

and his family regarding the engagement. He's so excited to finally meet and have you as his fiancée," he said. "How are you?"

"I'm okay. A little nervous about all of this. But I'll be alright."

"That's totally understandable. But I need you to know that Jun is a very nice guy and his family already adores you." He kissed my forehead.

I nodded. I didn't want to bring up the subject of Lyric as that would make this whole engagement more confusing, but a part of me wanted to tell my dad in private. I wanted to hope that he would understand why I didn't want to get engaged to Jun Lee. But I knew this was just wishful thinking. My whole family was on board with me marrying Jun and apparently his family was too. This was a battle I would never win. So why even try to press the issue of my love for Lyric?

My family and I sat in the living room to discuss the logistics of the engagement ceremony. The ceremony would last thirty minutes to an hour. After the ceremony, the two families would have a big traditional Chinese feast commencing our engagement. After we finished talking, my mom and dad said good night and went to their room. I was feeling tired and so was Mei, so we said good night to the others and went to our room.

In our room, Mei and I each put on our pajamas and climbed in the bed. She turned on the TV to a Chinese show because we both liked background noise to fall asleep to, though I didn't think I'd be getting much sleep with the engagement. I tried to fall asleep, but I just ended up staring at the ceiling. Lying there with nothing but my thoughts became too much, and I began to cry.

Mei heard and turned toward me. "Xenia, what's the matter?"

"I don't want to get engaged to him," I said through my tears.

"You really love Lyric, don't you?" Mei sat up on the bed and motioned for me to sit up.

"I really do. I hate the fact that you don't care about my feelings and haven't vouched for me. I supported you and Qiang when your parents had some apprehensions toward him." I sat up and looked her in the eyes.

"But this is different. It's not that I don't want to support you. I just haven't known how I would go about supporting you without threatening Qiang's and my relationship," she said.

"How would it threaten your relationship with Qiang?" I started fidgeting with the comforter on the bed.

"It took our parents quite a while to accept me wanting to marry Qiang. I thought if they knew I supported you and Lyric, they would disown us too."

"Really? That's what you've been thinking?" I asked annoyed.

"I really am sorry, Xen. I know it was wrong for me to think that. But I did. Now I can see how much you care and love Lyric. It's just a hard position to be in, you know?"

"I don't know what to even say," I said somberly.

"Maybe you'll end up loving him more than Lyric. You never know," Mei said.

"Maybe . . . But I can't really see that happening. My feelings for Lyric are too strong to let someone else in to love me the way she would have."

"But how do you know Jun won't love you like Lyric would have. Just give him a chance. You'll see," she said trying to reassure me.

I sighed and wiped the tears from my eyes. I knew Mei was trying to understand and I appreciated her for coming around, but she would never understand. Although Lyric and I had only spent two months together, those two months had felt like a lifetime. To have that kind of love stripped from you was excruciating. I'd be mourning her forever.

CHAPTER 11
Lyric

I t had been about a month since Xenia and I broke up. I couldn't get her out of my mind. She lied to me yet I couldn't stop thinking about her. Ironically, I had been dating Zane, well, going on dates with Zane. After our initial date, I'd felt conflicted that I'd just left him hanging on where we stood for a second date. So, I'd called Zane a week later and let him know that I would go out to dinner with him. For the most part, we've been casually dating, nothing serious.

While Sierra and I were watching a movie one afternoon, she asked, "How are you and Zane getting along?"

"We're doing okay," I said nonchalantly.

"Just okay? How was y'all's dinner date?"

"It was good. He took me out to this Ethiopian restaurant. The food was remarkable, and the ambience was chill, but . . ."

"But?" Sierra looked at me and cocked her head to the side.

I decided to tell her the truth. "He's not Xenia." I sighed. "I'm also afraid that Zane will find out he's just a rebound and that I'm leading him on with no possibility of a future together."

"Lyric, I really think you are living in a fantasy world. You are messing up an awesome dating experience with a fantastic guy. All because you want a woman who is probably already engaged and not thinking twice about you." Sierra laid it bare.

"But what if Xenia *is* thinking about me? What if she didn't go through with the engagement? What if she told her parents the truth about us?" I reasoned.

"That's a real long shot, Lyric. I honestly think you should move on from her. You should give Zane a chance."

"You really like Zane, don't you? Do you want to date him?" I asked facetiously.

"Yes, I do like him. For you." Sierra smiled.

"Okay, well I'm not holding my breath, but I guess I will give him a chance."

"Good. Zane is a great guy, and you are a great girl. I think you can really be happy with him, Lyric." She paused. "Hey, listen, I have to go into the shop later to do some straightening up and such. How about I finally draw that tattoo for you?"

I had been wanting a dance-inspired tattoo, but after Xenia, that had changed. Now I wanted to get a violin on my ankle. I wanted the memory of Xenia not only on my heart but also permanently inked on my skin. I didn't care if she moved on or was going to be engaged to someone else. She was still my first everything. I wanted to remember that, even if it would be painful to look at in a few years. Xenia was a memory I never wanted to forget, even if she forgot about me.

"Sure! I'm ready. Can you draw a violin surrounded by hearts?" I said.

"A violin? Umm . . . do you think that's a good idea?" She looked at me and cocked her head to the side. "Why don't you just stick with a dance-inspired tattoo? Something you won't regret getting later."

"I won't regret it. It's not like its Xenia's name. Plus, I do like classical music and the violin."

Sierra rolled her eyes. "More like the girl who plays the instrument."

"So will you do it?"

"I usually don't recommend my clients get a tattoo of a name or something that reminds them of an ex-boyfriend or ex-girlfriend. Is there any way I can change your mind?

"Nope," I told her confidently.

"Alright. Give me a minute to get ready. Then we'll head to the shop." Sierra went into her bedroom.

As soon as she disappeared to her room, I thought about the violin I was going to get tattooed on my skin. Xenia was already tattooed in my mind. Her touch was like a searing-hot iron burning through the pores of my skin. Her kiss was like soft flower petals blowing in the wind. Her eyes were an ocean of wonder that told the story of our love whenever I gazed into them. This tattoo would be like having a piece of her on me, even when she wasn't here physically.

Sierra came back into the living room. "Ready?"

"Yup," I said.

WHEN WE ARRIVED at the shop, Sierra told me to have a seat while she did her little tidying up. While she was busy doing her thing, I grabbed the book of tattoos. I thumbed through the pages, looking at all the intricate tattoo designs. Most of them were drawn by Sierra herself. Some were very detailed and others were minimalistic. But each one was unique, none found anywhere else. That's what made Sierra the most sought-after tattoo artist in New York City. People knew that they weren't coming to get a carbon-copy tattoo but an original one that no one else had.

As I was glancing at the very last pages in the book, Sierra came out of one of the rooms holding a piece of paper. She walked over to where I was sitting and handed the paper to me.

I was in awe of the tattoo she'd drawn for me. It was a rough sketch of a brown violin surrounded by pink and red hearts. "This is amazing," I said, almost breathless.

"You like it?" she asked.

"Like it? I love it!"

"Well then, are you ready to get tatted?" Sierra smirked.

I took a breath and held onto my resolve. "Yes, yes, I am."

We walked back to her tattoo room, and I laid down on the table while she got everything set up. When she was finally ready to begin, she told me to take a few deep breaths.

"On your ankle, right?" she asked.

"Yes, on my ankle." I raked my hand through my hair.

"Don't be nervous. It will just feel like pins and needles going across your skin. The buzzing sound is my gun. So try and relax. It's a pretty small tattoo, so it shouldn't take me that long to outline it and color it in," Sierra explained.

I took one more deep breath in and exhaled out. Sierra put the tattoo gun to my ankle and started. It didn't hurt that bad when she was doing the outline. But it did hurt a little more when she was coloring in the violin and the hearts around it. The whole process took about an hour. After she was finished, I couldn't stop admiring my new ankle tattoo. It was all I'd wanted and more.

"I love it, Sierra. Thank you!" I hugged her.

"You're very welcome."

"How much do I owe you?" I asked.

"Nothing. It's on the house. But I don't want you to come to me in a few years to tell me you want it removed," Sierra warned. "Deal?"

"Deal."

Sierra explained how to care for my new ink and the healing time. "So, it's fairly easy to care for your new tattoo," she said as she cleaned and bandaged my tattoo.

"It seems pretty simple," I said.

"All finished," she said.

"Thank you." I looked down at my bandaged tattoo.

I hopped down from the table while Sierra cleaned and sterilized the equipment. Then we walked out to the front.

"I have to tidy up one more room. Then we can leave to go back to the apartment."

"Okay, no problem."

Sierra disappeared into the room she was about to clean, and I sat on the black cushion bench in the front and waited for her to finish. As I was sitting there, my phone vibrated in my pocket. Figuring it was Zane, I was tempted to ignore it. I didn't feel like talking to him right now. But something inside me told me to check the message, so I did. To my surprise, it was Xenia.

> Xenia: Hey, Lyric. How are you doing? I was just thinking about you. I want to meet up at Café Ciel. Are you free tomorrow? It's cool if you're not. But I would really like to see you and catch up.

I had to read the message a few times for it to register. *Xenia wants to meet up at the café. Tomorrow? And she's been thinking about me? Maybe she didn't get engaged and wanted to give our relationship another shot. Can I trust her not to lead me on again? Do I want to see her? Do I want to hear what she has to say? Of course, I do. But I'm scared. I don't want to get hurt again.*

I reread the message again and swallowed hard before responding.

> Me: I'm doing okay. I would love to meet and catch up. What time tomorrow?

> Xenia: Great! How's 2 sound?

> Me: 2 is perfect, see you then.

I closed my messages and put my phone away. As soon as I looked up, I saw Sierra staring at me from across the room. "How long have you been standing there?" I asked.

"Long enough to see you contemplating in your head," she said. "That wasn't a text from Zane, was it?"

"Umm . . ."

"Shit, Lyric. That was Xenia, wasn't it?" Sierra put her hands on her hips.

"Yes, it was her."

"What did she want?"

"To meet and catch up," I said sheepishly.

"You're not going, are you?" Sierra asked.

"I am. I want to hear what she has to say. Maybe we can rekindle our relationship."

"Lyric, I really don't think it's a good idea. I don't want you to get hurt again."

"I know. I don't want to get hurt again either. I get it. But I have a feeling that something good will come out of this meeting."

"Are you totally sure about that?" Sierra said, unconvinced.

"Yeah. I appreciate that. But I can handle this on my own.

If we are meant to be, things will line up when I go see her," I reassured her.

"Okay, as long as you're sure." She looked resigned to my decision. "I'm finished up here, so we can get going."

"Sounds good. Thanks again for doing my tattoo. I absolutely love it!"

THE NEXT AFTERNOON, I sat on my bed, ready to meet up with Xenia. I only had an hour to go until I met her at the café. So for that hour, I mentally prepared myself for various outcomes. All the different scenarios of how this meeting would go swam heavily through my mind. *What if she is indeed engaged and just wants to come tell me that? How will I handle not being able to be with her ever again? But what if she didn't get engaged and wants to rekindle our relationship? What will I say? How will I react?* So many unanswered questions.

Ten minutes before it was time to leave to head to the café, I finally surrendered the outcome. Whatever was supposed to happen would happen. I was at peace with that. My phone buzzed; it was a text from Xenia. She was already waiting at the café for me to arrive. *She must really be eager to talk to me.* The thought made me lightheaded. I felt like I was floating on a cloud of happiness.

I texted Sierra that I was leaving to meet Xenia. She texted back and wished me luck. That was it. I got in my car and drove to the café.

Once there, I walked up to the front door and peeked inside. Xenia was sitting in the same spot as when we had our first date. She was wearing a sparkly red dress with red "Dorothy" heels. Her long black hair was down, and bright red lipstick covered her beautiful lips. *Why is she so dressed up? I thought she just wanted to talk to me.* She looked so sexy in this dress. The way it framed her body. *Mmm . . . Is that her point, to fucking try to turn me on?* It was working. I stood there for a minute and then walked into the café.

I walked over to where Xenia was. She glanced at me and smiled as I sat across from her. There were two glasses of water on the table. So I reached for my glass and took a sip.

"Thanks for meeting me," Xenia said.

"No problem. It's good to see you again." I smiled.

"It's good to see you again too." She blushed.

"So how have you been?"

"I've been okay. I recently got back from China." She paused then blurted, "I'm engaged to Jun."

I sunk my back against the chair and sighed. "Oh . . . umm . . . congratulations?"

"Thank you. I want to apologize for leading you on. I wish that things were different and I wasn't engaged." She sounded remorseful. "How have you been?"

"I've been better. I'm dating this guy named Zane."

"Oh . . . and how's that going?"

"It's going all right. Truth be told, he's not you." I looked deep into her black, almond-shaped eyes. They appeared glassy, like she was about to cry.

"I know what you mean." Xenia glanced away.

I grabbed her hand and squeezed it. "So, you're not happy?"

"No . . . I'm not." Xenia stared at her hand in mine. She gazed into my eyes as tears fell from hers. "I hate the fact that I didn't tell my dad the truth. That I don't want to marry Jun. I hate that I wasn't brave enough to tell him about you."

"Is it too late?" I reached over and gently wiped her tears away.

"I'm not married yet, so technically it's not too late. But I'm scared to tell them. I will be disowned."

"But you'll have me. Isn't that worth it? We can be together. We can be a family. I know it won't be like the one you grew up in. But we will create our own path, unique and special to us. I love you, Xenia." I still held her hand.

I looked up at Lyric and gave her a shy grin. I didn't really have the words to convey how much I needed to hear that she loved me. But I hoped the twinkle in my eyes was enough. "I had a long time to think while I was in China. Even though I went through with the engagement, I was just going through the motions. I don't love Jun." Xenia smiled through her tears. "I love you. I want to spend the rest of my life with you, Lyric. No matter what comes our way, I want to face it with you by my side." She leaned down and kissed my hand.

That kiss sent an electric shock through my skin. Of all the scenarios I'd imagined, I'd barely let myself hope that this one would become true.

"We can do this. It may be hard at first. But there is no one I want to be with more than you." I motioned for her to come over and sit beside me.

When she did, I put my arms around her and hugged her tightly. After a few moments like that, I went in and kissed Xenia on her lips. She kissed me back like she was making up for lost time. I felt her longing . . . her desperation. When we pulled away from the kiss, she laughed at me.

"What?" I asked.

"You have my lipstick on your lips." She smiled and grabbed a napkin off the table.

I chuckled, and she wiped the lipstick off my lips. At that moment, I knew it would be okay, that we would be okay. I put my forehead against hers. We both took a few deep breaths in and out.

"I'm going to tell my family about us," Xenia said, slightly above a whisper.

"Are you sure?"

"Yes, I'm sure. I need to do this." She sounded distressed.

I knew this decision was weighing heavy on her mind. We both knew what the outcome would most likely be. But we were ready to live and love authentically despite what anyone else thought.

CHAPTER 12

Xenia

It was almost noon. I was still tired from tossing and turning the night before. Today was the day. I was going to meet my parents, Aunt Tao, and Mei this afternoon to discuss the plans for my upcoming weddings. The family, Jun Lee, and I decided to have a yearlong engagement. I would marry when I was twenty-six. The plan was to have a traditional wedding in China and an American wedding in New York. Today was the day we were going to get the ball rolling with the planning of both weddings. What my parents didn't know was that I was about to drop a bomb on them and tell them about Lyric. I would confess that I loved her and wanted to be with her instead of marrying Jun. But I was nervous as hell. *After I tell my parents, I'll probably have to live forever without them.*

I couldn't believe I was actually going to finally tell my parents about us. The whole morning, Lyric had been sending encouraging texts. She knew how stressed I was. Lyric was kind of sneaky too. She would send naughty pictures of herself between the texts meant to encourage me. I didn't know what I was going to do with her. She was a therapist and a sexy siren all wrapped in one package. I still couldn't believe I got to call her my girlfriend. Jun Lee definitely had nothing on Lyric. She was one of a kind and all mine.

I was simultaneously stressed and nervous, so I decided to jot down my thoughts before heading to meet my parents. Even though I knew the outcome of making my confession, it didn't take away from the fact that I had to actually tell them. I was going to have to witness their reactions in real time and have that memory forever etched in my mind. I was sure I could have thought of other ways of telling them so I wouldn't have to witness their reactions. But I'd rather speak with my parents face-to-face than over text. It would lessen the blow, but it was the right thing to do. It was heartbreaking to know that this would likely be the final interaction I would ever have with my parents.

After writing down my thoughts, I dressed and ate something. I decided to shoot Lyric a text.

> Me: Hey Lyric, I'm going to head to my parents' house in a few minutes.

> Lyric: Okay, please don't worry. No matter the outcome, I will always be here for you. I love you.

I appreciated my girlfriend so much. For her to be so caring and loyal to me after the shit I'd put her through said a lot. I would never make that mistake again, nor ever take Lyric for granted again.

I arrived at my parents' house around 1 p.m. We all sat in the living room. My mom had a notebook and pen to take notes. Mei had her laptop open to take notes and research wedding-related information. Aunt Tao sat in as the mediator for what was being said, and my dad was there to approve the budget for the whole thing.

"I'm so glad we're all here to get the wedding planning process started," my mom began. "The engagement ceremony was an absolute success, so I expect nothing less for the weddings."

"I've been looking at some venues for the New York wedding," Mei said. "I found a few worth looking at."

"I also found some places in China to have the traditional wedding," my dad explained. "During the week I was there, I talked with Jun's family, especially his sisters, about wedding venues. The ones we found were reasonably priced and very beautiful."

I sat there, listening to my family talk through all the specifics about the venues for my weddings. I just nodded and agreed with what they were saying. I was there, but my heart and mind were elsewhere. Suddenly, my hands started to feel clammy, and my hearing started to get muffled. I felt hot all over. It was like I was witnessing them talking from outside of my body.

Mei looked up from her computer. "Are you okay, Xenia?" she asked loudly.

My mom and Aunt Tao glanced at me. I must have looked like I was about to die because Aunt Tao rushed over and fanned me with the notebook that my mom had been taking notes in.

"Hurry up and bring the water," Aunt Tao yelled at my mom, who had already run into the kitchen. "Just breathe, Xenia."

I took a few deep breaths, in and out. Soon my mom was back in the living room, trying to get me to drink the water.

"Xen, what's wrong?" my mom asked as she stroked my hair.

"If this is too much for you to handle, we can schedule this meeting for another day," my dad interjected.

Everyone started to say their piece about whether we should continue with this meeting, going back and forth. It was almost like I wasn't even there.

"Wait . . . wait . . . Stop it!" I yelled.

They halted their conversation and glanced in my direction.

"Honey, you don't have to—" my mom started to say.

"Yes, Mom, I do," I said, cutting her off. I looked around the room at my family. They were all sitting, looking at me, silent. "Ever since you guys began planning this engagement ceremony, you never asked me once what I thought or even if I wanted to marry Jun," I started.

"Xenia," Mei said as a warning. She knew what I was getting ready to tell them, but I wasn't going to back down now.

"Well, you were hardly around, and we needed to start thinking about this," my mom said.

"You should have asked me, told me, reached out, anything. I could have made time," I said.

"We also knew that your career as a violinist took up most of your time," Aunt Tao interjected.

"These are all excuses," I said.

"So, you don't want to marry Jun?" my dad asked.

"No, Dad. I don't. I've met someone and I want to be with them."

"You have? Why didn't you tell us this earlier?" my mom asked. "You know we would have accepted the gentleman that you chose. We learned from the mistake we made with Mei choosing Qiang and not accepting him at first."

"Umm . . . I'm afraid it's not that simple." I sighed and looked down.

"How is it not simple?" Aunt Tao questioned.

"Xenia, are you sure you want to tell them?" Mei said with trepidation in her voice.

"Tell us what?" my mom asked, giving me a look of bewilderment.

It was now or never. I looked around the room at each one of their questioning faces. Mei glared at me, shook her head, and mouthed, *Don't tell them.*

"The guy that I want to be with isn't a guy," I said.

Looks of confusion blanketed their faces. Aunt Tao let out a nervous laugh, and everyone continued to look at me in silence.

This was a lot harder than I'd expected. I wasn't sure how to proceed. I didn't know if I wanted to. But I couldn't let Lyric down. I had to tell them about her. I didn't want to marry Jun and that was the truth. I took a deep breath, glancing at each of them one by one. I knew the next thing I was going to say would change the trajectory of our lives forever.

"I'm in love with a woman, and her name is Lyric," I blurted.

My mom, dad, and Aunt Tao looked at me with shock and horror in their eyes. Then they proceeded to look at each other like, *Is she serious?*

"Is this some sort of joke?" my mom asked.

"It's no joke, Mom. She's very creative, compassionate, and we—" I started to say.

"You won't be doing anything with her in this house," my dad said angrily, cutting me off.

"I knew this would probably be your reaction," I said somberly.

"Then why don't you save yourself the heartache and just marry Jun?" Mei said, then quickly drew back in her seat.

"You knew about this . . . this love affair between them?" My mom looked at Mei with disbelief.

"Umm . . . I . . . I . . ." she said nervously.

"We'll speak to you later," my dad said to Mei with sternness in his voice. "How long have you been seeing this girl, Xenia?"

"For a while now."

"Was it before you got engaged to Jun?" He clenched his jaw.

"Yes. I wanted to tell you about her when we were in China. But I didn't have the courage to."

"And what made you tell us now?"

"Because she's my girlfriend and I don't want to marry Jun." I sat as tall as I could.

"I see." Dad rubbed his face with both hands and scratched at his whiskers for a moment. "I can call off the engagement with Jun Lee. But as long as you and her are together, you won't be allowed in this house. We don't know what's gotten into you. We didn't raise you this way."

I listened to my dad's words ricochet off the walls of the house. I didn't have anything else to say. I had said all I was going to. I'd accepted this as my fate when I'd chosen to rekindle my relationship with Lyric.

"Xen, why?" my mom asked, tears in her eyes. "There are tons of guys you could have dated if you didn't want to marry Jun. We would have been welcoming to him. But this . . . with a woman . . . absolutely not."

"I'm sorry, Mom. I can't help who I love." My heart felt like it was crumbling onto the floor. I looked around the room at my family. "I'm going to go now." Tears swam in my eyes. I got up off the couch and walked to the front door. I glanced back into the living room at them one last time. Then I left.

As soon as I got back to my apartment, I went to my room. I laid across my bed and started crying uncontrollably. I hadn't realized know how much this confession would take out of me. I felt like the wind had been knocked out of me. It felt hard to breathe, knowing that the world as I knew it now would be no longer. *How will I make it?* I wondered. *How will we ever make it?* We couldn't survive on our love alone. We needed support; we needed guidance. We couldn't do this on our own.

When I finally composed myself, I searched online for some LGBTQ+ resources Lyric and I could lean on. If nothing else, I knew I had Brielle. She'd been supportive of our relationship since I'd told her about it. Lyric was visiting her parents, so I couldn't call to let her know what happened. I hoped her conversation went better than mine had.

When I finished looking up some resources, I wrote myself a letter. I wanted to remember the details of what had transpired this afternoon with my family. Even if I never read this letter again or eventually ripped it to shreds, at least I could get what I was feeling down on paper. When I finished writing, I folded the paper into a square and put it in my nightstand drawer. Not knowing what else to do, I ventured into the living room to watch some TV. As soon as I sat on my couch and settled on a show, there was a knock on my door.

"Who in the world?" I mumbled as I got up to get the door.

When I opened my front door, there sat a bouquet of red roses and a box of chocolates. I picked them up, carried them inside, and set them on my kitchen counter.

A small envelope was attached to the bouquet. I ripped open the envelope and took out a note:

> Xenia,
>
> I'm so very proud of you. You are one of the bravest humans I've ever met. You fought for us even though you knew it would cost you everything you've ever known. But in reality, even though you lost, you also gained. You gained me, your girlfriend and forever love. I will be eternally grateful for everything we had to lose. Because it allowed us to access what we have now, what we will have later, and what we will have in the future. I love you so very much!
>
> —Lyric

Tears ran down my face. I had the sweetest girlfriend. I didn't deserve her. Yet, I had her and she wanted me. Despite my flaws and the way I'd treated her, she still wanted to give me another chance. I was forever indebted to this woman. I knew we were going to build the best life together, regardless of any opposition, now or in the future.

Epilogue

LYRIC

THREE MONTHS LATER

It has been two weeks since I moved into Xenia's apartment. Sierra had decided to stay at the apartment. Both Sierra and Brielle had helped us move my things into Xenia's apartment. I was so thankful to have Sierra and Brielle in our lives. I wouldn't have known who to turn to if it weren't for them. Soon after Xenia told her parents about our relationship, I told my parents about us. They weren't happy to say the least. I haven't talked to my parents since I'd told them about Xenia. They'd basically stated I was no longer their daughter. They'd said they needed some time and space to figure out if they wanted me and Xenia to be in their lives. The funny thing was that you would think that my parents would have been more open-minded being that they both worked in the entertainment industry. But unfortunately, that hadn't been the case.

One night after dance practice, I came home feeling emotionally drained. When I walked in the front door of our apartment, I was surprised to see Xenia holding a blindfold.

"What the hell is this?" I asked confused.

She tied the blindfold over my eyes. "Shh, baby. Let me take the lead," Xenia whispered in my ear.

She led me through our apartment. There was soft music playing.

"I'm going to sit you down here," Xenia said, gently guiding me. As I sat, it felt soft and plush.

"Now lie down," she said.

As soon as I was flat on my back, Xenia started to undo my jeans and pull them, along with my panties, off.

"What are you doing?" I couldn't see anything through the blindfold.

"Getting ready to fuck you senseless," she said.

A few seconds later, I heard a buzzing noise. I stiffened, my body going tense.

"Relax, baby," she said softly. "It's a vibrator."

I felt the vibrator run across my toes. "That tickles," I said, giggling.

I heard her gasp and felt her lips kiss my ankle. "When did you get this tattoo? It's beautiful," she said.

"Right before we got back together. I wanted to get a tattoo to remind me of you."

"Did it hurt?" she asked.

"It was a mixture of pain and pleasure."

"That's so fucking sexy. How about I give you a mixture of pain and pleasure?" she growled.

I bit my bottom lip. Xenia slowly moved the vibrator up my thigh, inching closer to my clit. When I felt the toy teasing my entrance, I took a deep breath in. As I went to exhale, Xenia pushed the toy deep in me with one thrust.

"Holy shit," I screamed.

She worked the vibrator inside me. I bucked my hips and

started grinding against the toy. A few minutes later, I felt Xenia's body against mine. She removed my blindfold, and then she immediately came down and kissed me hard.

Naked herself, she inserted the other end of the toy inside of her, and we started fucking each other. Beads of sweat formed on our bodies as we moved with the rhythm of the toy.

After a good while of having sex, she removed the toy from us.

"Here, babe." She put her end of the toy to my lips.

I took her end into my mouth. I wanted to remember how she tasted since the last time we had sex. Oh my God, Xenia tasted like heaven on earth.

"Mmm . . ." I moaned and took the toy out of my mouth.

"You are music to my ears, Lyric," she said. "Now it's my turn." Xenia put my end of the vibrator in her mouth and sucked on it. "Oh, babe, I could taste you forever."

THE NEXT MORNING, I got up while Xenia was still in bed and made us breakfast. While I waited for Xenia to get up, I sat at the table with some tea. Sipping my tea, I thought about the wild ride Xenia and I had been on in the past few months. In some ways, it was extremely difficult not having either of our families in our lives. We both had had close relationships with our parents. Even though we knew it could happen, to have that suddenly ripped from us, I didn't think we were really emotionally prepared to face that level of grief. It has been heart-wrenching. So much so that we recently started seeing a therapist, which had been great.

Aside from grieving the loss of family, we were so happy

that we were together at last. I wouldn't trade it for the world. Being able to wake up next to Xenia every day had been the highlight of this whole difficult situation. Plus the fact that I was able to forgive her so quickly. It was probably a shock to her that I was able to. It was even a shock to me. But I loved Xenia too much to withhold forgiveness from her.

As I continued to sip my tea, I heard footsteps coming down the hall.

"Morning, baby," Xenia said as she came over and kissed my forehead.

She was wearing a white silk robe with tiny little rainbows scattered all over it and matching silk slippers. The robe was silk and kind of see-through. She was only wearing the red lace bra and panties she'd worn to bed last night.

"Morning, love, I made us breakfast," I said proudly.

"I could smell the food from inside our bedroom. The aroma tickled my nose and woke me up." Xenia started to fix herself a plate. "I can fix your plate too, if you want?"

"Sure. Thanks, darling," I said.

When she was finished, she brought both plates to the table and sat down. "Brielle texted me to see if we wanted to go out tonight," Xenia said after taking a sip of her orange juice.

"Oh really? What did you say? A night out sounds fun."

"I told her we had to finish a few things around the apartment. But we would definitely be up for going out tonight. She also told me to tell you to invite Sierra."

"I'm sure Sierra would love to come out with us. Where are we going?" I asked.

"She said there's an upscale lesbian bar and lounge, Rainbow Elite, that she wants to try."

"I never heard of that place before. She must have looked

it up." I smiled. "We must be rubbing off on our straight friends."

"I guess we are." Xenia laughed.

I loved Xenia's laugh. I could listen to it for hours. It was so infectious. It always put me in a great mood as soon as I heard it. It also turned me on so fucking much.

"What do we have to do around the apartment?" I asked.

"Remember we talked about putting the flag up above our headboard?"

"Oh yeah. Maybe after we finish eating, we can start on that," I suggested.

"Sounds like a plan."

I texted Sierra and asked her if she wanted to go to Rainbow Elite with us tonight. I told her that it would be with me, Xen, and Brielle. I really needed a girls' night, especially after everything we'd gone through these past couple of months.

We finished eating and went into the bedroom to tackle the mission of hanging the lesbian flag above our headboard. Together, we spread the flag flat against the wall above our bed and tacked it into place. Then we tacked a few pictures of us to the inside of the flag. For the finishing touch, we hung a border of white lights around it.

"What did Sierra say about going out with us?" Xenia asked as we sat on our bed admiring our work.

I checked my phone. "She said that sounds perfect and that she needs a night out after the stress of work."

"Okay, awesome. So the next thing is . . . what are we going to wear?" Xenia asked, obviously excited.

"It won't be hard to find something to wear between the both of us," I said.

"I guess that's the perk of being in a lesbian relationship," she said with a little laugh.

"That's a definite perk." I laughed along with her.

WE MET Sierra and Brielle at the lounge. I chose to wear a black sequined halter top, dark-wash flare jeans, and black sparkly block heels. I convinced Xenia to wear that red dress with the red sparkly "Dorothy" heels that she wore the last time we met up at the café. She had curled her hair a little too. She looked so fucking sexy in that dress, I couldn't take my eyes off of her.

The lounge was pretty packed. Even though I wasn't really much of a club goer, the atmosphere seemed very chill and laid-back. There were a ton of women on the dance floor, hand in hand, swaying to the beat of the music. Other women were grabbing drinks at the bar or chatting it up with one another at their tables.

"Sorry, we're just getting here," Sierra said walking up to our table. "I got stuck at work, so I called Brielle to come and help me bail."

"Yeah, I had to talk Everly into closing the shop for her," Brielle said.

"No worries, you're here now," I said.

Brielle and Sierra both sat at the table, and we all ordered drinks and some food. As soon as the server left, Brielle and Xenia got up to go to the dance floor.

"Hey, no stealing my girlfriend," I said to Brielle jokingly.

Xenia looked back at me. "There's no way. I'm yours forever."

"You really got lucky with that one there," Sierra said as she watched me gaze at my girlfriend.

"Can you believe I almost lost her to Jun?" I asked.

"She would have come back to you eventually. So how's it going living together?"

"Like a literal dream. Picture waking up to your best friend every morning. It's a feeling like no other in the world," I told her.

"And your parents . . . have they reached out to you?"

"My parents actually just called the other day, but I haven't called them back yet," I said.

A few months had passed since I told my parents about Xenia. They had a while to think, and thankfully, they came around. Maybe they realized that even though I'm not with the man they envisioned me with, that I could still be happy. And I am extremely happy with the life I'm building with Xenia.

"That's wonderful. Maybe they're coming around. How about Xenia's parents?"

"Unfortunately, Xenia hasn't spoken to her parents." I took a sip of my water.

"How are you and her dealing with that?" Sierra asked.

"We actually both started going to therapy. It's helped both of us deal with the emptiness of not being in connection with our families," I explained.

"Do you think your families will eventually come around?" She put her elbows on the table and leaned forward, looking straight into my eyes.

"My family might, at least that's what I'm hoping, but I can't say the same for Xenia's parents. But even if her parents never talk to her again, I'll be there for Xenia. I will always be there for her. I made that promise and I intend to keep it."

The food came, and Xenia and Brielle returned to the table. Xenia sat next to me and embraced me. We held on tightly to each other.

Xenia leaned in. "We'll be okay, no matter what," she

whispered in my ear. "As long as we have each other, that's all we need."

I looked at the women with me around the table, and I knew it was true. This was my chosen family, and come hell or high water, I knew I'd always have them.

Acknowledgments

Stacey at One Word Editing:
It was such a pleasure to work with you on Lyrical Symphony. You made me realize how much I've grown in my writing skills as an author and for that I thank you.

Diana TC:
You definitely get the vision I have for the covers of my books and bring it to life. I appreciate you so much, thank you for making me yet another EPIC cover for Lyrical Symphony

Jo McCall: Thank you so much designing the beautiful interior for Lyrical Symphony.

Family and Friends:
Thank you so much for the continued support of me and my books. I love you all.

About the Author

Regina Ann Faith *is a Lyricist, Poet, Writer, and Author. She graduated with a B.A in Communications/Film. Lyrical Symphony is a new adult interracial sapphic romance. It's the love story between Lyric, a professional dancer and Xenia, a professional violinist who both always dated guys. They end up developing feelings each other but never anticipated it would turn into something more.*

She can be found on her social media pages at:
 @reginaannfaith
 Facebook
 Twitter
 Instagram
 TikTok

www.ingramcontent.com/pod-product-compliance
Lightning Source LLC
Chambersburg PA
CBHW020622250626
47154CB00004B/1623